THE NEW WINDMILL SERIES

General Editors: Anne and Ian Serraillier

71

THE KITE

AND OTHER STORIES

This is a collection of some of Somerset Maugham's finest stories. The longest, *The Kite*, is the subtle story of a young man's obsessive attachment to kite-flying; the others include a spy story set in Switzerland, a ghost story set in Spain, a character sketch of an Italian fisherman, and a story of a man who on the day he was to be married ran away from the girl who had come six thousand miles to marry him.

W. SOMERSET MAUGHAM

The Kite

and other stories

INTRODUCED BY
IAN SERRAILLIER

HEINEMANN EDUCATIONAL

BOOKS LTD · LONDON

Heinemann Educational Books Ltd

LONDON   EDINBURGH   MELBOURNE   TORONTO
SINGAPORE   JOHANNESBURG
HONG KONG   AUCKLAND
IBADAN   NAIROBI

SBN 435 12071 9

Introduction © Ian Serraillier 1963
The complete short stories of W. Somerset Maugham
are published by William Heinemann Ltd in three
volumes.
This edition first published 1963
Reprinted 1965, 1967, 1969 (twice)

Published by Heinemann Educational Books Ltd
48 Charles Street, London W1X 8AH
Printed and bound in Great Britain by
Bookprint Limited, Crawley, Sussex

Contents

Introduction

SOMERSET MAUGHAM was born in 1874. He lived in Paris until he was ten, by which time both his mother and his father had died. With no proper home for him in France, he was sent to Whitstable in Kent to live with his uncle, who was vicar there. Lonely, shy and often unwell, he missed in the vicarage the affectionate atmosphere his parents had created for him. At The King's School, Canterbury, he was no happier, but a year spent at Heidelberg University with brief visits to Italy and Switzerland was more successful. It gave him a sense of freedom, a love of travel which was never to leave him, and a determination to become a writer.

The idea of a literary career did not appeal to his uncle, who agreed however to his studying medicine. At St Thomas's Hospital the eighteen-year-old student gave more time to reading and writing than to his medical studies, and he filled notebooks with ideas for stories and plays. Later on he found the out-patients' department and also the maternity work in the slums of Lambeth more interesting. He felt he was now in contact with what he most wanted, life in the raw, and this gave him some knowledge of human nature. 'In those years,' he wrote, 'I must have witnessed pretty well every emotion of which man is capable. It appealed to my dramatic instinct. It excited the novelist in me.'

His first novel, *Liza of Lambeth*, published in his final year at medical school, reflected some of these experiences. Though he did not make much money out of it, he nevertheless decided against practising as a doctor, and after wandering through

Spain and Italy he settled down in Paris with a group of artists and writers to continue his professional literary career.

Finding that he had little gift for fine writing and that 'poetic flights and the great imaginative sweep' were beyond his scope, he taught himself to write clearly, simply and euphoniously. His keen powers of observation, his feeling for language, and above all his instinct for a good story all stood him in good stead, and as he planned his work quite deliberately with an eye to success with a wide public, it was not long before he began to reap the benefits. In a working life that spanned more than six decades he has won fame as a novelist, critic, essayist and travel writer. He became one of the most successful of British playwrights on the London stage, as well as the most popular writer of short stories of the century. It is with these that we are concerned here.

The abundant supply of popular magazines, almost all of which have now vanished, made it natural for an Edwardian author with Maugham's gifts to use the medium of the short story. Today radio, cinema and television have extended his audience to millions, and some of the stories in the present collection will be familiar to many who have never read them. One of the best of them, *The Kite*, was a highly successful and effective film. This study of a lower middle-class family and the break-up of a marriage is very modern in feeling as well as in its acute perception of the workings of the mind. Most of the stories date back to the period between the two world wars, and when Maugham writes of 'before the war' he means before 1914–18. During the first world war he worked for a while as a secret agent in the Intelligence Department. Much of the work was monotonous, and the material it could offer him for stories was scrappy and pointless. Nevertheless, by making it, as he says, 'coherent, dramatic and probable' he was able to use it as a basis for his six *Ashenden* stories. Of these, *The Traitor*, a precise and moving account of the trapping of a German spy, is a powerful example. The writing is much more detached than in most other spy stories of the period. There is no suggestion that German spies are more treacherous than the British; to betray your country for money is a pretty poor business whatever side you happen to be on. What was it then that made a kindly jovial man of modest tastes and deeply attached to his wife turn traitor? The author's main interest is in the spy's motives as well as in his relationship with the dull and humourless yet devoted woman who was his wife. He tells the story without heroics and at a leisurely pace, but with a controlled tension that grips the reader from start to finish.

Control and compactness are a feature of all Maugham's stories, however long or short, whether they are violent, tragic, or humorous and light. They are neatly shaped, with a beginning, a middle and an end, and he makes constant use of surprise. How did *The Man with the Scar* get his disfigurement? The opening paragraph suggests an obvious answer, but for the true one we have to wait till the end. All except one of the stories in this selection are written in the first person. This is a literary convention as old as the hills. 'Its object,' Maugham says, 'is of course to achieve credibility, for when someone tells you what he states happened to himself you are more likely to believe that he is telling the truth than when he tells you what happened to somebody else.' The *I* who writes is not a faithful portrait of the author himself. He may be the hero, an onlooker, or a confidant; but he is always just as much a character in the story as other people in it.

And it is with people that Maugham is primarily concerned. For the most part they are not ordinary, decent, normal people living humdrum lives, but people with some singularity of temperament or character – an illiterate Londoner who made a fortune in business, a merchant who behaved ruthlessly though he looked too kind to hurt a fly, a man who on the day he was to be married ran away from the girl who had come six thousand miles to marry him. In *Salvatore* he accomplishes the difficult feat of writing a moving and credible story about a man who was completely selfless. The settings may be in England, Switzerland, Japan, the Far East, or any place that Maugham has visited. (On page 134 the reader will find a glossary of foreign words.) A great traveller, he never stayed anywhere for long without finding material for one or more tales. It is this basis of fact, made entertaining by the skill of the story-teller, that makes them so plausible.

Critical opinion about Maugham's work is divided and, as often happens with a popular writer, his easy readability has sometimes told against him. But this has not dismayed him, for he takes a modest view of his powers. Whatever his ultimate position may be, the fact remains that already two generations of readers the world over have warmly appreciated his stories, and they continue to be enjoyed by an ever widening circle.

Somerset Maugham died at his home in the South of France in December 1965.

IAN SERRAILLIER

Acknowledgments:

W. Somerset Maugham   *The Summing Up*
Prefaces to *The Complete Short Stories*

Richard Cordell   *Somerset Maugham*
A biographical and critical study

Home

THE farm lay in a hollow among the Somersetshire hills, an old-fashioned stone house surrounded by barns and pens and outhouses. Over the doorway the date when it was built had been carved in the elegant figures of the period, 1673, and the house, grey and weather-beaten, looked as much a part of the landscape as the trees that sheltered it. An avenue of splendid elms that would have been the pride of many a squire's mansion led from the road to the trim garden. The people who lived here were as stolid, sturdy and unpretentious as the house; their only boast was that ever since it was built from father to son in one unbroken line they had been born and died in it. For three hundred years they had farmed the surrounding land. George Meadows was now a man of fifty, and his wife was a year or two younger. They were both fine, upstanding people in the prime of life; and their children, two sons and three girls, were handsome and strong. They had no newfangled notions about being gentlemen and ladies; they knew their place and were proud of it. I have never seen a more united household. They were merry, industrious and kindly. Their life was patriarchal. It had a completeness that gave it a beauty as definite as that of a symphony by Beethoven or a picture by Titian. They were happy and they deserved their happiness. But the master of the house was not George Meadows (not by a long chalk, they said in the village); it was his mother. She was twice the man her son was, they said. She was a woman of seventy, tall, upright and dignified, with grey hair, and though her face was much wrinkled, her eyes were bright and shrewd. Her word was law in the house and on the farm; but she had humour, and if her rule was despotic it was also kindly. People laughed at her jokes and repeated them. She was a good business woman and you had to get up very early in the morning to best her in a bargain. She was a character. She combined in a rare degree good will with an alert sense of the ridiculous.

One day Mrs George stopped me on my way home. She was all in a flutter. (Her mother-in-law was the only Mrs Meadows we knew; George's wife was only known as Mrs George.)

'Whoever do you think is coming here today?' she asked me. 'Uncle George Meadows. You know, him as was in China.'

'Why, I thought he was dead.'

'We all thought he was dead.'

I had heard the story of Uncle George Meadows a dozen times, and it had amused me because it had the savour of an old ballad: it was oddly touching to come across it in real life. For Uncle George Meadows and Tom, his younger brother, had both courted Mrs Meadows when she was Emily Green, fifty years and more ago, and when she married Tom, George had gone away to sea.

They heard of him on the China coast. For twenty years now and then he sent them presents; then there was no more news of him; when Tom Meadows died his widow wrote and told him, but received no answer; and at last they came to the conclusion that he must be dead. But two or three days ago to their astonishment they had received a letter from the matron of the sailors' home at Portsmouth. It appeared that for the last ten years George Meadows, crippled with rheumatism, had been an inmate and now, feeling that he had not much longer to live, wanted to see once more the house in which he was born. Albert Meadows, his great-nephew, had gone over to Portsmouth in the Ford to fetch him and he was to arrive that afternoon.

'Just fancy,' said Mrs George, 'he's not been here for more

than fifty years. He's never even seen my George, who's fifty-one next birthday.'

'And what does Mrs Meadows think of it?' I asked.

'Well, you know what she is. She sits there and smiles to herself. All she says is, "He was a good-looking young fellow when he left, but not so steady as his brother." That's why she chose my George's father. "But he's probably quietened down by now," she says.'

Mrs George asked me to look in and see him. With the simplicity of a country woman who had never been farther from her home than London, she thought that because we had both been in China we must have something in common. Of course I accepted. I found the whole family assembled when I arrived; they were sitting in the great old kitchen, with its stone floor, Mrs Meadows in her usual chair by the fire, very upright, and I was amused to see that she had put on her best silk dress, while her son and his wife sat at the table with their children. On the other side of the fireplace sat an old man, bunched up in a chair. He was very thin and his skin hung on his bones like an old suit much too large for him; his face was wrinkled and yellow and he had lost nearly all his teeth.

I shook hands with him.

'Well, I'm glad to see you've got here safely, Mr Meadows,' I said.

'Captain,' he corrected.

'He walked here,' Albert, his great-nephew, told me. 'When he got to the gate he made me stop the car and said he wanted to walk.'

'And mind you, I've not been out of my bed for two years. They carried me down and put me in the car. I thought I'd never walk again, but when I see them elm trees, I remember my father set a lot of store by them elm trees, I felt I could walk. I walked down that drive fifty-two years ago when I went away and now I've walked back again.'

'Silly, I call it,' said Mrs Meadows.

'It's done me good. I feel better and stronger than I have for ten years. I'll see you out yet, Emily.'

'Don't you be too sure,' she answered.

I suppose no one had called Mrs Meadows by her first name for a generation. It gave me a little shock, as though the old man were taking a liberty with her. She looked at him with a shrewd smile in her eyes and he, talking to her, grinned with his tooth-less gums. It was strange to look at them, these two old people who had not seen one another for half a century, and to think that all that long time ago he had loved her and she had loved another. I wondered if they remembered what they had felt then and what they had said to one another. I wondered if it seemed to him strange now that for that old woman he had left the home of his fathers, his lawful inheritance, and lived an exile's life.

'Have you ever been married, Captain Meadows?' I asked.

'Not me,' he said, in his quavering voice, with a grin. 'I know too much about women for that.'

'That's what you say,' retorted Mrs Meadows. 'If the truth was known I shouldn't be surprised to hear as how you'd had half a dozen black wives in your day.'

'They're not black in China, Emily, you ought to know better than that, they're yellow.'

'Perhaps that's why you've got so yellow yourself. When I saw you, I said to myself, why, he's got jaundice.'

'I said I'd never marry anyone but you, Emily, and I never have.'

He said this not with pathos or resentment, but as a mere state-ment of fact, as a man might say, 'I said I'd walk twenty miles and I've done it.' There was a trace of satisfaction in the speech.

'Well, you might have regretted it if you had,' she answered.

I talked a little with the old man about China.

'There's not a port in China that I don't know better than you know your coat pocket. Where a ship can go I've been. I could keep you sitting here all day long for six months and not tell you half the things I've seen in my day.'

'Well, one thing you've not done, George, as far as I can see,' said Mrs Meadows, the mocking but not unkindly smile still in her eyes, 'and that's to make a fortune.'

'I'm not one to save money. Make it and spend it; that's my motto. But one thing I can say for myself: if I had the chance of going through my life again I'd take it. And there's not many as'll say that.'

'No, indeed,' I said.

I looked at him with admiration and respect. He was a tooth-less, crippled, penniless old man, but he had made a success of life, for he had enjoyed it. When I left him he asked me to come and see him again next day. If I was interested in China he would tell me all the stories I wanted to hear.

Next morning I thought I would go and ask if the old man would like to see me. I strolled down the magnificent avenue of elm trees and when I came to the garden saw Mrs Meadows picking flowers. I bade her good morning and she raised herself. She had a huge armful of white flowers. I glanced at the house and I saw that the blinds were drawn: I was surprised, for Mrs Meadows liked the sunshine.

'Time enough to live in the dark when you're buried,' she always said.

'How's Captain Meadows?' I asked her.

'He always was a harum-scarum fellow,' she answered. 'When Lizzie took him a cup of tea this morning she found he was dead.'

'Dead?'

'Yes. Died in his sleep. I was just picking these flowers to put in the room. Well, I'm glad he died in that old house. It always means a lot to them Meadows to do that.'

They had had a good deal of difficulty in persuading him to

go to bed. He had talked to them of all the things that had happened to him in his long life. He was happy to be back in his old home. He was proud that he had walked up the drive without assistance, and he boasted that he would live for another twenty years. But fate had been kind: death had written the full-stop in the right place.

Mrs Meadows smelt the white flowers that she held in her arms.

'Well, I'm glad he came back,' she said. 'After I married Tom Meadows and George went away, the fact is I was never quite sure that I'd married the right one.'

A Man from Glasgow

It is not often that anyone entering a great city for the first time has the luck to witness such an incident as engaged Shelley's attention when he drove into Naples. A youth ran out of a shop pursued by a man armed with a knife. The man overtook him and with one blow in the neck laid him dead on the road. Shelley had a tender heart. He didn't look upon it as a bit of local colour; he was seized with horror and indignation. But when he expressed his emotions to a Calabrian priest who was travelling with him, a fellow of gigantic strength and stature, the priest laughed heartily and attempted to quiz him. Shelley says he never felt such an inclination to beat anyone.

I have never seen anything so exciting as that, but the first time I went to Algeciras I had an experience that seemed to me far from ordinary. Algeciras was then an untidy, neglected town. I arrived somewhat late at night and went to an inn on the quay. It was rather shabby, but it had a fine view of Gibraltar, solid and matter-of-fact, across the bay. The moon was full. The office was on the first floor, and a slatternly maid, when I asked for a room, took me upstairs. The landlord was playing cards. He seemed little pleased to see me. He looked me up and down, curtly gave me a number, and then, taking no further notice of me, went on with his game.

When the maid had shown me to my room I asked her what I could have to eat.

'What you like,' she answered.

I knew well enough the unreality of the seeming profusion.

'What have you got in the house?'

'You can have eggs and ham.'

The look of the hotel had led me to guess that I should get little else. The maid led me to a narrow room with whitewashed walls and a low ceiling in which was a long table laid already for the next day's luncheon. With his back to the door sat a tall man, huddled over a *brasero*, the round brass dish of hot ashes which is erroneously supposed to give sufficient warmth for the temperate winter of Andalusia. I sat down at table and waited for my scanty meal. I gave the stranger an idle glance. He was looking at me, but meeting my eyes he quickly turned away. I waited for my eggs. When at last the maid brought them he looked up again.

'I want you to wake me in time for the first boat,' he said.

'*Si, señor.*'

His accent told me that English was his native tongue, and the breadth of his build, his strongly marked features, led me to suppose him a northerner. The hardy Scot is far more often found in Spain than the Englishman. Whether you go to the rich mines of Rio Tinto, or to the bodegas of Jerez, to Seville or to Cadiz, it is the leisurely speech of beyond the Tweed that you hear. You will meet Scotsmen in the olive groves of Carmona, on the railway between Algeciras and Bobadilla, and even in the remote cork woods of Merida.

I finished eating and went over to the dish of burning ashes. It was midwinter and the windy passage across the bay had chilled my blood. The man pushed his chair away as I drew mine forwards.

'Don't move,' I said. 'There's heaps of room for two.'

I lit a cigar and offered one to him. In Spain the Havana from Gib is never unwelcome.

'I don't mind if I do,' he said, stretching out his hand.

I recognized the singing speech of Glasgow. But the stranger was not talkative, and my efforts at conversation broke down before his monosyllables. We smoked in silence. He was even bigger than I had thought, with great broad shoulders and ungainly limbs; his face was sunburned, his hair short and grizzled. His features were hard; mouth, ears and nose were large and heavy and his skin much wrinkled. His blue eyes were pale. He was constantly pulling his ragged, grey moustache. It was a nervous gesture that I found faintly irritating. Presently I felt that he was looking at me, and the intensity of his stare grew so irksome that I glanced up expecting him, as before, to drop his eyes. He did, indeed, for a moment, but then raised them again. He inspected me from under his long, bushy eyebrows.

'Just come from Gib?' he asked suddenly.

'Yes.'

'I'm going tomorrow – on my way home. Thank God.'

He said the last two words so fiercely that I smiled.

'Don't you like Spain?'

'Oh, Spain's all right.'

'Have you been here long?'

'Too long. Too long.'

He spoke with a kind of gasp. I was surprised at the emotion my casual inquiry seemed to excite in him. He sprang to his feet and walked backwards and forwards. He stamped to and fro like a caged beast, pushing aside a chair that stood in his way, and now and again repeated the words in a groan. 'Too long. Too long.' I sat still. I was embarrassed. To give myself countenance I stirred the *brasero* to bring the hotter ashes to the top, and he stood suddenly still, towering over me, as though my movement had brought back my existence to his notice. Then he sat down heavily in his chair.

'D'you think I'm queer?' he asked.

'Not more than most people,' I smiled.

'You don't see anything strange in me?'

He leant forward as he spoke so that I might see him well.

'No.'

'You'd say so if you did, wouldn't you?'

'I would.'

I couldn't quite understand what all this meant. I wondered if he was drunk. For two or three minutes he didn't say anything and I had no wish to interrupt the silence.

'What's your name?' he asked suddenly. I told him.

'Mine's Robert Morrison.'

'Scotch?'

'Glasgow. I've been in this blasted country for years. Got any baccy?'

I gave him my pouch and he filled his pipe. He lit it from a piece of burning charcoal.

'I can't stay any longer. I've stayed too long. Too long.'

He had an impulse to jump up again and walk up and down, but he resisted it, clinging to his chair. I saw on his face the effort he was making. I judged that his restlessness was due to chronic alcoholism. I find drunks very boring, and I made up my mind to take an early opportunity of slipping off to bed.

'I've been managing some olive groves,' he went on. 'I'm here working for the Glasgow and South of Spain Olive Oil Company Limited.'

'Oh, yes.'

'We've got a new process for refining oil, you know. Properly treated, Spanish oil is every bit as good as Lucca. And we can sell it cheaper.'

He spoke in a dry, matter-of-fact, business-like way. He chose his words with Scotch precision. He seemed perfectly sober.

'You know, Ecija is more or less the centre of the olive trade, and we had a Spaniard there to look after the business. But I found he was robbing us right and left, so I had to turn him out. I used to live in Seville; it was more convenient for shipping the oil. However, I found I couldn't get a trustworthy man to be at Ecija, so last year I went there myself. D'you know it?'

'No.'

'The firm has got a big estate two miles from the town, just outside the village of San Lorenzo, and it's got a fine house on it. It's on the crest of a hill, rather pretty to look at, all white, you know, and straggling, with a couple of storks perched on the roof. No one lived there, and I thought it would save the rent of a place in town if I did.'

'It must have been a bit lonely,' I remarked.

'It was.'

Robert Morrison smoked on for a minute or two in silence. I wondered whether there was any point in what he was telling me.

I looked at my watch.

'In a hurry?' he asked sharply.

'Not particularly. It's getting late.'

'Well, what of it?'

'I suppose you didn't see many people?' I said, going back.

'Not many. I lived there with an old man and his wife who looked after me, and sometimes I used to go down to the village and play *tresillo* with Fernandez, the chemist, and one or two men who met at his shop. I used to shoot a bit and ride.'

'It doesn't sound such a bad life to me.'

'I'd been there two years last spring. By God, I've never known such heat as we had in May. No one could do a thing. The labourers just lay about in the shade and slept. Sheep died and some of the animals went mad. Even the oxen couldn't work. They stood around with their backs all humped up and gasped for breath. That blasted sun beat down and the glare was so awful, you felt your eyes would shoot out of your head. The earth cracked and crumbled, and the crops frizzled. The olives went to rack and ruin. It was simply hell. One couldn't get a wink of sleep. I went from room to room, trying to get a breath of air. Of course I kept the windows shut and had the floors watered, but that didn't do any good. The nights were just as hot as the days. It was like living in an oven.

'At last I thought I'd have a bed made up for me downstairs on the north side of the house in a room that was never used because in ordinary weather it was damp. I had an idea that I might get a few hours' sleep there at all events. Anyhow it was worth trying. But it was no damned good; it was a washout. I turned and tossed and my bed was so hot that I couldn't stand it. I got up and opened the doors that led to the veranda and walked out. It was a glorious night. The moon was so bright that I swear you could read a book by it. Did I tell you the house was on the crest of a hill? I leant against the parapet and looked at the olive trees. It was like the sea. I suppose that's what made me think of home. I thought of the cool breeze in the fir trees and the racket of the streets in Glasgow. Believe it or not, I could smell them, and I could smell the sea. By God, I'd have given every bob I had in the world for an hour of that air. They say it's a foul climate in Glasgow. Don't you believe it. I like the rain and the grey sky and that yellow sea and the waves. I forgot that I was in Spain, in the middle of the olive country, and I opened my mouth and took a long breath as though I were breathing-in the sea-fog.

'And then all of a sudden I heard a sound. It was a man's voice. Not loud, you know, low. It seemed to creep through the silence like – well, I don't know what it was like. It surprised me. I couldn't think who could be down there in the olives at that hour. It was past midnight. It was a chap laughing. A funny sort of laugh. I suppose you'd call it a chuckle. It seemed to crawl up the hill – disjointedly.'

Morrison looked at me to see how I took the odd word he used to express a sensation that he didn't know how to describe.

'I mean, it seemed to shoot up in little jerks, something like shooting stones out of a pail. I leant forward and stared. With the full moon it was almost as light as day, but I'm dashed if I could see a thing. The sound stopped, but I kept on looking at where it had come from in case somebody moved. And in a minute it started off again, but louder. You couldn't have called it a chuckle any more, it was a real belly laugh. It just rang through the night. I wondered it didn't wake my servants. It sounded like someone who was roaring drunk.

' "Who's there?" I shouted.

'The only answer I got was a roar of laughter. I don't mind telling you I was getting a bit annoyed. I had half a mind to go down and see what it was all about. I wasn't going to let some drunken swine kick up a row like that on my place in the middle of the night. And then suddenly there was a yell. By God, I was startled. Then cries. The man had laughed with a deep bass voice, but his cries were – shrill, like a pig having his throat cut.

' "My God," I cried.

'I jumped over the parapet and ran down towards the sound. I thought somebody was being killed. There was silence and then one piercing shriek. After that sobbing and moaning. I'll tell you what it sounded like, it sounded like someone at the point of death. There was a long groan and then nothing. Silence. I ran from place to place. I couldn't find anyone. At last I climbed the hill again and went back to my room.

'You can imagine how much sleep I got that night. As soon as it was light, I looked out of the window in the direction from which the row had come and I was surprised to see a little white house in a sort of dale among the olives. The ground on that side didn't belong to us and I'd never been through it. I hardly ever went to that part of the house and so I'd never seen the house before. I asked José who lived there. He told me that a madman had inhabited it, with his brother and a servant.'

'Oh, was that the explanation?' I said. 'Not a very nice neighbour.'

The Scot bent over quickly and seized my wrist. He thrust his face into mine and his eyes were starting out of his head with terror.

'The madman had been dead for twenty years,' he whispered. He let go my wrist and leant back in his chair panting.

'I went down to the house and walked all round it. The windows were barred and shuttered and the door was locked. I knocked. I shook the handle and rang the bell. I heard it tinkle, but no one came. It was a two-storey house and I looked up. The shutters were tight closed, and there wasn't a sign of life anywhere.'

'Well, what sort of condition was the house in?' I asked.

'Oh, rotten. The whitewash had worn off the walls and there was practically no paint left on the door or the shutters. Some of the tiles off the roof were lying on the ground. They looked as though they'd been blown away in a gale.'

'Queer,' I said.

'I went to my friend Fernandez, the chemist, and he told me the same story as José. I asked about the madman and Fernandez said that no one ever saw him. He was more or less comatose ordinarily, but now and then he had an attack of acute mania and then he could be heard from ever so far laughing his head off and then crying. It used to scare people. He died in one of his attacks and his keepers cleared out at once. No one had ever dared to live in the house since.

'I didn't tell Fernandez what I'd heard. I thought he'd only laugh at me. I stayed up that night and kept watch. But nothing happened. There wasn't a sound. I waited about till dawn and then I went to bed.'

'And you never heard anything more?'

'Not for a month. The drought continued and I went on sleeping in the lumber-room at the back. One night I was fast asleep, when something seemed to happen to me; I don't exactly know how to describe it, it was a funny feeling as though someone had given me a little nudge, to warn me, and suddenly I was wide awake. I lay there in my bed and then in the same way as before I heard a long, low gurgle, like a man enjoying an old joke.

It came from away down in the valley and it got louder. It was a great bellow of laughter. I jumped out of bed and went to the window. My legs began to tremble. It was horrible to stand there and listen to the shouts of laughter that rang through the night. Then there was the pause, and after that a shriek of pain and that ghastly sobbing. It didn't sound human. I mean, you might have thought it was an animal being tortured. I don't mind telling you I was scared stiff. I couldn't have moved if I'd wanted to. After a time the sounds stopped, not suddenly, but dying away little by little. I strained my ears, but I couldn't hear a thing. I crept back to bed and hid my face.

'I remembered then that Fernandez had told me that the madman's attacks only came at intervals. The rest of the time he was quite quiet. Apathetic, Fernandez said. I wondered if the fits of mania came regularly. I reckoned out how long it had been between the two attacks I'd heard. Twenty-eight days. It didn't take me long to put two and two together; it was quite obvious that it was the full moon that set him off. I'm not a nervous man really and I made up my mind to get to the bottom of it, so I looked out in the calendar which day the moon would be full next and that night I didn't go to bed. I cleaned my revolver and loaded it. I prepared a lantern and sat down on the parapet of my house to wait. I felt perfectly cool. To tell you the truth, I was rather pleased with myself because I didn't feel scared. There was a bit of a wind, and it whistled about the roof. It rustled over the leaves of the olive trees like waves swishing on the pebbles of the beach. The moon shone on the white walls of the house in the hollow. I felt particularly cheery.

'At last I heard a little sound, the sound I knew, and I almost laughed. I was right; it was the full moon and the attacks came as regular as clockwork. That was all to the good. I threw myself over the wall into the olive grove and ran straight to the house. The chuckling grew louder as I came near. I got to the house and looked up. There was no light anywhere. I put my

ears to the door and listened. I heard the madman simply laughing his damned head off. I beat on the door with my fist and I
pulled the bell. The sound of it seemed to amuse him. He roared
with laughter. I knocked again, louder and louder, and the more
I knocked the more he laughed. Then I shouted at the top of
my voice.

' "Open the blasted door, or I'll break it down."

'I stepped back and kicked the latch with all my might. I
flung myself at the door with the whole weight of my body.
It cracked. Then I put all my strength into it and the damned
thing smashed open.

'I took the revolver out of my pocket and held my lantern in
the other hand. The laughter sounded louder now that the door
was opened. I stepped in. The stink nearly knocked me down.
I mean, just think, the windows hadn't been opened for twenty
years. The row was enough to raise the dead, but for a moment
I didn't know where it was coming from. The walls seemed to
throw the sound backwards and forwards. I pushed open a door
by my side and went into a room. It was bare and white and
there wasn't a stick of furniture in it. The sound was louder
and I followed it. I went into another room, but there was
nothing there. I opened a door and found myself at the foot of
a staircase. The madman was laughing just over my head. I
walked up, cautiously, you know, I wasn't taking any risks,
and at the top of the stairs there was a passage. I walked along
it, throwing my light ahead of me, and I came to a room at the
end. I stopped. He was in there. I was only separated from the
sound by a thin door.

'It was awful to hear it. A shiver passed through me and I
cursed myself because I began to tremble. It wasn't like a human
being at all. By Jove, I very nearly took to my heels and ran. I
had to clench my teeth to force myself to stay. But I simply
couldn't bring myself to turn the handle. And then the laughter
was cut, cut with a knife you'd have said, and I heard a hiss of

pain. I hadn't heard that before, it was too low to carry to my place, and then a gasp.

' "Ay!" I heard the man speak in Spanish. "You're killing me. Take it away. O God, help me!"

'He screamed. The brutes were torturing him. I flung open the door and burst in. The draught blew a shutter back and the moon streamed in so bright that it dimmed my lantern. In my ears, as clearly as I hear you speak and as close, I heard the wretched chap's groans. It was awful, moaning and sobbing, and frightful gasps. No one could survive that. He was at the point of death. I tell you I heard his broken, choking cries right in my ears. And the room was empty.'

Robert Morrison sank back in his chair. That huge solid man had strangely the look of a lay figure in a studio. You felt that if you pushed him he would fall over in a heap on to the floor.

'And then?' I asked.

He took a rather dirty handkerchief out of his pocket and wiped his forehead.

'I felt I didn't much want to sleep in that room on the north side, so, heat or no heat, I moved back to my own quarters. Well, exactly four weeks later, about two in the morning, I was waked up by the madman's chuckle. It was almost at my elbow. I don't mind telling you that my nerve was a bit shaken by then, so next time the blighter was due to have an attack, next time the moon was full, I mean, I got Fernandez to come and spend the night with me. I didn't tell him anything. I kept him up playing cards till two in the morning, and then I heard it again. I asked him if he heard anything. "Nothing," he said. "There's somebody laughing," I said. "You're drunk, man," he said, and he began laughing too. That was too much. "Shut up, you fool," I said. The laughter grew louder and louder. I cried out. I tried to shut it out by putting my hands to my ears, but it wasn't a damned bit of good. I heard it and I heard the scream of pain. Fernandez thought I was mad. He didn't dare say so, because he knew I'd have killed him. He said he'd go to bed, and in the morning I found he'd slunk away. His bed hadn't been slept in. He'd taken himself off when he left me.

'After that I couldn't stop in Ecija. I put a factor there and went back to Seville. I felt myself pretty safe there, but as the time came near I began to get scared. Of course I told myself not to be a damned fool, but, you know, I damned well couldn't help myself. The fact is, I was afraid the sounds had followed me, and I knew if I heard them in Seville I'd go on hearing them all my life. I've got as much courage as any man, but damn it all, there are limits to everything. Flesh and blood couldn't stand it. I knew I'd go stark staring mad. I got in such a state that I began drinking, the suspense was so awful, and I used to lie awake counting the days. And at last I knew it'd come. And it came. I heard those sounds in Seville – sixty miles away from Ecija.'

I didn't know what to say. I was silent for a while.

'When did you hear the sounds last?' I asked.

'Four weeks ago.'

I looked up quickly. I was startled.

'What d'you mean by that? It's not full moon tonight?'

He gave me a dark, angry look. He opened his mouth to speak and then stopped as though he couldn't. You would have said his vocal cords were paralysed, and it was with a strange croak that at last he answered.

'Yes, it is.'

He stared at me and his pale blue eyes seemed to shine red. I have never seen in a man's face a look of such terror. He got up quickly and stalked out of the room, slamming the door behind him.

I must admit that I didn't sleep any too well that night myself.

The Man with the Scar

IT was on account of the scar that I first noticed him, for it
ran, broad and red, in a great crescent from his temple to his
chin. It must have been due to a formidable wound and I
wondered whether this had been caused by a sabre or by a frag-
ment of shell. It was unexpected on that round, fat and good-
humoured face. He had small and undistinguished features, and
his expression was artless. His face went oddly with his
corpulent body. He was a powerful man of more than common
height. I never saw him in anything but a very shabby grey
suit, a khaki shirt and a battered sombrero. He was far from
clean. He used to come into the Palace Hotel at Guatemala City
every day at cocktail time and strolling leisurely round the bar
offer lottery tickets for sale. If this was the way he made his
living it must have been a poor one for I never saw anyone buy,
but now and then I saw him offered a drink. He never refused
it. He threaded his way among the tables with a sort of rolling
walk as though he were accustomed to traverse long distances
on foot, paused at each table, with a little smile mentioned the
numbers he had for sale and then, when no notice was taken of
him, with the same smile passed on. I think he was for the most
part a trifle the worse for liquor.

I was standing at the bar one evening, my foot on the rail,
with an acquaintance – they make a very good dry Martini at
the Palace Hotel in Guatemala City – when the man with the
scar came up. I shook my head as for the twentieth time since
my arrival he held out for my inspection his lottery tickets.
But my companion nodded affably.

'*Qué tal, general?* How is life?'

'Not so bad. Business is none too good, but it might be worse.'

'What will you have, general?'

'A brandy.'

He tossed it down and put the glass back on the bar. He nodded to my acquaintance.

'*Gracias. Hasta luego.*'

Then he turned away and offered his tickets to the men who were standing next to us.

'Who is your friend?' I asked. 'That's a terrific scar on his face.'

'It doesn't add to his beauty, does it? He's an exile from Nicaragua. He's a ruffian of course and a bandit, but not a bad fellow. I give him a few *pesos* now and then. He was a revolutionary general, and if his ammunition hadn't given out he'd have upset the government and be Minister of War now instead of selling lottery tickets in Guatemala. They captured him, along with his staff, such as it was, and tried him by court-martial. Such things are rather summary in these countries, you know, and he was sentenced to be shot at dawn. I guess he knew what was coming to him when he was caught. He spent the night in gaol and he and the others, there were five of them altogether, passed the time playing poker. They used matches for chips. He told me he'd never had such a run of bad luck in his life; they were playing with a short pack, Jacks to open, but he never held a card; he never improved more than half a dozen times in the whole sitting and no sooner did he buy a new stack than he lost it. When day broke and the soldiers came into the cell to fetch them for execution he had lost more matches than a reasonable man could use in a lifetime.

'They were led into the patio of the gaol and placed against a wall, the five of them side by side, with the firing-party facing them. There was a pause and our friend asked the officer in charge of them what the devil they were keeping him waiting

for. The officer said that the general commanding the government troops wished to attend the execution and they awaited
his arrival.

' "Then I have time to smoke another cigarette," said our
friend. "He was always unpunctual."

'But he had barely lit it when the general – it was San Ignacio,
by the way: I don't know whether you ever met him – followed
by his A.D.C. came into the patio. The usual formalities were
performed and San Ignacio asked the condemned men whether
there was anything they wished before the execution took place.
Four of the five shook their heads, but our friend spoke.

' "Yes, I should like to say good-bye to my wife."

' "*Bueno*," said the general, "I have no objection to that.
Where is she?"

' "She is waiting at the prison door."

' "Then it will not cause a delay of more than five minutes."

' "Hardly that, *Señor General*," said our friend.

' "Have him placed on one side."

'Two soldiers advanced and between them the condemned
rebel walked to the spot indicated. The officer in command of
the firing-squad on a nod from the general gave an order, there
was a ragged report, and the four men fell. They fell strangely,
not together, but one after the other, with movements that were
almost grotesque, as though they were puppets in a toy theatre.
The officer went up to them and into one who was still alive
emptied two barrels of his revolver. Our friend finished his
cigarette and threw away the stub.

'There was a little stir at the gateway. A woman came into
the patio, with quick steps, and then, her hand on her heart,
stopped suddenly. She gave a cry and with outstretched arms
ran forward.

' "*Caramba*," said the General.

'She was in black, with a veil over her hair, and her face was
dead white. She was hardly more than a girl, a slim creature,

with little regular features and enormous eyes. But they were distraught with anguish. Her loveliness was such that as she ran, her mouth slightly open and the agony of her face beautiful, a gasp of surprise was wrung from those indifferent soldiers who looked at her.

'The rebel advanced a step or two to meet her. She flung herself into his arms and with a hoarse cry of passion: *alma de mi corazón*, soul of my heart, he pressed his lips to hers. And at the same moment he drew a knife from his ragged shirt — I haven't a notion how he managed to retain possession of it — and stabbed her in the neck. The blood spurted from the cut vein and dyed his shirt. Then he flung his arms round her and once more pressed his lips to hers.

'It happened so quickly that many did not know what had occurred, but from the others burst a cry of horror; they sprang forward and seized him. They loosened his grasp and the girl would have fallen if the A.D.C. had not caught her. She was unconscious. They laid her on the ground and with dismay on their faces stood round watching her. The rebel knew where he was striking and it was impossible to staunch the blood. In a moment the A.D.C. who had been kneeling by her side rose.

' "She's dead," he whispered.

'The rebel crossed himself.

' "Why did you do it?" asked the general.

' "I loved her."

'A sort of sigh passed through those men crowded together and they looked with strange faces at the murderer. The general stared at him for a while in silence.

' "It was a noble gesture," he said at last. "I cannot execute this man. Take my car and have him led to the frontier. *Señor*, I offer you the homage which is due from one brave man to another."

'A murmur of approbation broke from those who listened.

The A.D.C. tapped the rebel on the shoulder, and between the two soldiers without a word he marched to the waiting car.'

My friend stopped and for a little I was silent. I must explain that he was a Guatemalecan and spoke to me in Spanish. I have translated what he told me as well as I could, but I have made no attempt to tone down his rather high-flown language. To tell the truth I think it suits the story.

'But how then did he get the scar?' I asked at length.

'Oh, that was due to a bottle that burst when I was opening it. A bottle of ginger ale.'

'I never liked it,' said I.

The Traitor

W HEN Ashenden, given charge of a number of spies working from Switzerland, was first sent there, R., wishing him to see the sort of reports that he would be required to obtain, handed him the communications, a sheaf of typewritten documents, of a man known in the Secret Service as Gustav.

'He's the best fellow we've got,' said R. 'His information is always very full and circumstantial. I want you to give his reports your very best attention. Of course Gustav is a clever little chap, but there's no reason why we shouldn't get just as good reports from the other agents. It's merely a question of explaining exactly what we want.'

Gustav, who lived at Basle, represented a Swiss firm with branches at Frankfort, Mannheim and Cologne, and by virtue of his business was able to go in and out of Germany without risk. He travelled up and down the Rhine, and gathered material about the movement of troops, the manufacture of munitions, the state of mind of the country (a point on which R. laid stress) and other matters upon which the Allies desired information. His frequent letters to his wife hid an ingenious code and the moment she received them in Basle she sent them to Ashenden in Geneva, who extracted from them the important facts and communicated these in the proper quarter. Every two months Gustav came home and prepared one of the reports that served as models to the other spies in this particular section of the Secret Service.

His employers were pleased with Gustav and Gustav had reason to be pleased with his employers. His services were so useful that he was not only paid more highly than the others, but for particular scoops had received from time to time a handsome bonus.

This went on for more than a year. Then something aroused R.'s quick suspicions; he was a man of an amazing alertness, not so much of mind, as of instinct, and he had suddenly a feeling that some hanky-panky was going on. He said nothing definite to Ashenden (whatever R. surmised he was disposed to keep to himself), but told him to go to Basle, Gustav being then in Germany, and have a talk with Gustav's wife. He left it to Ashenden to decide the tenor of the conversation.

Having arrived at Basle, and leaving his bag at the station, for he did not yet know whether he would have to stay or not, he took a tram to the corner of the street in which Gustav lived and, with a quick look to see that he was not followed, walked along to the house he sought. It was a block of flats that gave you the impression of decent poverty and Ashenden conjectured that they were inhabited by clerks and small tradespeople. Just inside the door was a cobbler's shop and Ashenden stopped.

'Does Herr Grabow live here?' he asked in his none too fluent German.

'Yes, I saw him go up a few minutes ago. You'll find him in.'

Ashenden was startled, for he had but the day before received through Gustav's wife a letter addressed from Mannheim in which Gustav by means of his code gave the numbers of certain regiments that had just crossed the Rhine. Ashenden thought it unwise to ask the cobbler the question that rose to his lips, so thanked him and went up to the third floor, on which he knew already that Gustav lived. He rang the bell and heard it tinkle within. In a moment the door was opened by a dapper little man with a close-shaven round head and spectacles. He wore carpet slippers.

'Herr Grabow?' asked Ashenden.

'At your service,' said Gustav.

'May I come in?'

Gustav was standing with his back to the light and Ashenden could not see the look on his face. He felt a momentary hesitation and gave the name under which he received Gustav's letters from Germany.

'Come in, come in. I am very glad to see you.'

Gustav led the way into a stuffy little room, heavy with carved oak furniture, and on the large table covered with a table-cloth of green velveteen was a typewriter. Gustav was apparently engaged in composing one of his invaluable reports. A woman was sitting at the open window darning socks, but at a word from Gustav rose, gathered up her things and left. Ashenden had disturbed a pretty picture of connubial bliss.

'Sit down, please. How very fortunate that I was in Basle! I have long wanted to make your acquaintance. I have only just this minute returned from Germany.' He pointed to the sheets of paper by the typewriter. 'I think you will be pleased with the news I bring. I have some very valuable information.' He chuckled. 'One is never sorry to earn a bonus.'

He was very cordial, but to Ashenden his cordiality rang false. Gustav kept his eyes, smiling behind the glassᵤ, fixed watchfully on Ashenden, and it was possible that they held a trace of nervousness.

'You must have travelled quickly to get here only a few hours after your letter, sent here and then sent on by your wife, reached me in Geneva.'

'That is very probable. One of the things I had to tell you is that the Germans suspect that information is getting through by means of commercial letters and so they have decided to hold up all mail at the frontier for eight-and-forty hours.'

'I see,' said Ashenden amiably. 'And was it on that account

that you took the precaution of dating your letter forty-eight hours after you sent it?'

'Did I do that? That was very stupid of me. I must have mistaken the day of the month.'

Ashenden looked at Gustav with a smile. That was very thin; Gustav, a business man, knew too well how important in his particular job was the exactness of a date. The circuitous routes by which it was necessary to get information from Germany made it difficult to transmit news quickly and it was essential to know precisely on what days certain events had taken place.

'Let me look at your passport a minute,' said Ashenden.

'What do you want with my passport?'

'I want to see when you went into Germany and when you came out.'

'But you do not imagine that my comings and goings are marked on my passport? I have methods of crossing the frontier.'

Ashenden knew a good deal of this matter. He knew that both the Germans and the Swiss guarded the frontier with severity.

'Oh? Why should you not cross in the ordinary way? You were engaged because your connection with a Swiss firm supplying necessary goods to Germany made it easy for you to travel backwards and forwards without suspicion. I can understand that you might get past the German sentries with the connivance of the Germans, but what about the Swiss?'

Gustav assumed a look of indignation.

'I do not understand you. Do you mean to suggest that I am in the service of the Germans? I give you my word of honour . . . I will not allow my integrity to be impugned.'

'You would not be the only one to take money from both sides and provide information of value to neither.'

'Do you pretend that my information is of no value? Why then have you given me more bonuses than any other agent has received? The Colonel has repeatedly expressed the highest satisfaction with my services.'

It was Ashenden's turn now to be cordial.

'Come, come, my dear fellow, do not try to ride the high horse. You do not wish to show me your passport and I will not insist. You are not under the impression that we leave the statements of our agents without corroboration or that we are so foolish as not to keep track of their movements? Even the best of jokes cannot bear an indefinite repetition. I am in peace-time a humorist by profession and I tell you that from bitter experience.' Now Ashenden thought the moment had arrived to attempt his bluff; he knew something of the excellent but diffi-cult game of poker. 'We have information that you have not been to Germany now, nor since you were engaged by us, but have sat here quietly in Basle, and all your reports are merely due to your fertile imagination.'

Gustav looked at Ashenden and saw a face expressive of nothing but tolerance and good-humour. A smile slowly broke on his lips and he gave his shoulders a little shrug.

'Did you think I was such a fool as to risk my life for fifty pounds a month? I love my wife.'

Ashenden laughed outright.

'I congratulate you. It is not everyone who can flatter himself that he has made a fool of our Secret Service for a year.'

'I had the chance of earning money without any difficulty. My firm stopped sending me into Germany at the beginning of the war, but I learned what I could from the other travellers. I kept my ears open in restaurants and beer-cellars, and I read the German papers. I got a lot of amusement out of sending you reports and letters.'

'I don't wonder,' said Ashenden.

'What are you going to do?'

'Nothing. What can we do? You are not under the impression that we shall continue to pay you a salary?'

'No, I cannot expect that.'

'By the way, if it is not indiscreet, may I ask if you have been playing the same game with the Germans?'

'Oh, no,' Gustav cried vehemently. 'How can you think it? My sympathies are absolutely pro-Ally. My heart is entirely with you.'

'Well, why not?' asked Ashenden. 'The Germans have all the money in the world and there is no reason why you should not get some of it. We could give you information from time to time that the Germans would be prepared to pay for.'

Gustav drummed his fingers on the table. He took up a sheet of the now useless report.

'The Germans are dangerous people to meddle with.'

'You are a very intelligent man. And after all, even if your salary is stopped, you can always earn a bonus by bringing us news that can be useful to us. But it will have to be substantiated; in future we pay only by results.'

'I will think of it.'

For a moment or two Ashenden left Gustav to his reflections. He lit a cigarette and watched the smoke he had inhaled fade into the air. He thought too.

'Is there anything particular you want to know?' asked Gustav suddenly.

Ashenden smiled.

'It would be worth a couple of thousand Swiss francs to you if you could tell me what the Germans are doing with a spy of theirs in Lucerne. He is an Englishman and his name is Grantley Caypor.'

'I have heard the name,' said Gustav. He paused a moment. 'How long are you staying here?'

'As long as necessary. I will take a room at the hotel and let you know the number. If you have anything to say to me you can be sure of finding me in my room at nine every morning and at seven every night.'

'I should not risk coming to the hotel. But I can write.'

'Very well.'

Ashenden rose to go and Gustav accompanied him to the door. 'We part without ill-feeling then?' he asked.

'Of course. Your reports will remain in our archives as models of what a report should be.'

Ashenden spent two or three days visiting Basle. It did not much amuse him. He passed a good deal of time in the book-shops turning over the pages of books that would have been worth reading if life were a thousand years long. Once he saw Gustav in the street. On the fourth morning a letter was brought up with his coffee. The envelope was that of a commercial firm unknown to him and inside it was a typewritten sheet. There was no address and no signature. Ashenden wondered if Gustav was aware that a typewriter could betray its owner as certainly as a handwriting. Having twice carefully read the letter, he held the paper up to the light to see the watermark (he had no reason for doing this except that the sleuths of detective novels always did it), then struck a match and watched it burn. He scrunched up the charred fragments in his hand.

He got up, for he had taken advantage of his situation to breakfast in bed, packed his bag and took the next train to Berne. From there he was able to send a code telegram to R. His instructions were given to him verbally two days later, in the bedroom of his hotel at an hour when no one was likely to be seen walking along a corridor, and within twenty-four hours, though by a circuitous route, he arrived at Lucerne.

Having taken a room at the hotel at which he had been in-structed to stay, Ashenden went out; it was a lovely day, early in August, and the sun shone in an unclouded sky. He had not been to Lucerne since he was a boy and but vaguely remem-bered a covered bridge, a great stone lion and a church in which he had sat, bored yet impressed, while they played an organ;

and, now wandering along a shady quay (and the lake looked just as tawdry and unreal as it looked on the picture-postcards) he tried not so much to find his way about a half-forgotten scene as to reform in his mind some recollection of the shy and eager lad, so impatient for life (which he saw not in the present of his adolescence but only in the future of his manhood) who so long ago had wandered there. But it seemed to him that the most vivid of his memories was not of himself, but of the crowd; he seemed to remember sun and heat and people; the train was crowded and so was the hotel, the lake steamers were packed and on the quays and in the streets you threaded your way among the throng of holiday-makers. They were fat and old and ugly and odd, and they stank. Now, in war-time, Lucerne was as deserted as it must have been before the world at large dis-covered that Switzerland was the playground of Europe. Most of the hotels were closed, the streets were empty, the rowing-boats for hire rocked idly at the water's edge and there was none to take them, and in the avenues by the lake the only persons to be seen were serious Swiss taking their neutrality, like a dachshund, for a walk with them. Ashenden felt exhilarated by the solitude and, sitting down on a bench that faced the water, surrendered himself deliberately to the sensation. It was true that the lake was absurd, the water was too blue, the mountains too snowy, and its beauty, hitting you in the face, exasperated rather than thrilled; but all the same there was something pleasing in the prospect, an artless candour, like one of Mendelssohn's *Songs Without Words*, that made Ashenden smile with complacency. Lucerne reminded him of wax flowers under glass cases and cuckoo clocks and fancy-work in Berlin wool. So long at all events as the fine weather lasted he was prepared to enjoy himself. He did not see why he should not at least try to combine pleasure to himself with profit to his country. He was travelling with a brand-new passport in his pocket, under a borrowed name, and this gave him an agreeable sense of owning a new personality. He was often slightly tired of himself and it diverted him for a while to be merely a creature of R.'s facile invention. The experience he had just enjoyed appealed to his acute sense of the absurd. R., it is true, had not seen the fun of it: what humour R. possessed was of a sardonic turn and he had no facility for taking in good part a joke at his own expense. To do that you must be able to look at yourself from the outside and be at the same time spectator and actor in the pleasant comedy of life. R. was a soldier and regarded introspection as unhealthy, un-English and unpatriotic.

Ashenden got up and strolled slowly to his hotel. It was a small German hotel, of the second class, spotlessly clean, and his bedroom had a nice view; it was furnished with brightly varnished pitch-pine, and though on a cold wet day it would have been wretched, in that warm and sunny weather it was gay and pleasing. There were tables in the hall and he sat down at one of these and ordered a bottle of beer. The landlady was curious to know why in that dead season he had come to stay and he was glad to satisfy her curiosity. He told her that he had recently recovered from an attack of typhoid and had come to Lucerne to get back his strength. He was employed in the Censorship Department and was taking the opportunity to brush up his rusty German. He asked her if she could recommend to him a German teacher. The landlady was a blond and blowsy Swiss, good-humoured and talkative, so that Ashenden felt pretty sure that she would repeat in the proper quarter the information he gave her. It was his turn now to ask a few questions. She was voluble on the subject of the war on account of which the hotel, in that month so full that rooms had to be found for visitors in neighbouring houses, was nearly empty. A few people came in from outside to eat their meals *en pension* but she had only two lots of resident guests. One was an old Irish couple who lived in Vevey and passed their summers in Lucerne and the other was an Englishman and his wife. She was a German and they were obliged on that account to live in a neutral country. Ashenden took care to show little curiosity about them – he recognized in the description Grantley Caypor – but of her own accord she told him that they spent most of the day walking about the mountains. Herr Caypor was a botanist and much interested in the flora of the country. His lady was a very nice woman and she felt her position keenly. Ah, well, the war could not last for ever. The landlady bustled away and Ashenden went upstairs.

Dinner was at seven, and, wishing to be in the dining-room before anyone else so that he could take stock of his fellow-guests as they entered, he went down as soon as he heard the bell. It was a very plain, stiff, whitewashed room, with chairs of the same shiny pitch-pine as in his bedroom, and on the walls were oleographs of Swiss lakes. On each little table was a bunch of flowers. It was all neat and clean and presaged a bad dinner. Ashenden would have liked to make up for it by ordering a bottle of the best Rhine wine to be found in the hotel, but did not venture to draw attention to himself by extravagance (he saw on two or three tables half-empty bottles of table hock, which made him surmise that his fellow-guests drank thriftily), and so contented himself with ordering a pint of lager. Presently one or two persons came in, single men with some occupation in Lucerne and obviously Swiss, and sat down each at his own little table and untied the napkins that at the end of luncheon they had neatly tied up. They propped newspapers against their water-jugs and read while they somewhat noisily ate their soup. Then entered a very old tall bent man, with white hair and a drooping white moustache, accompanied by a little old white-haired lady in black. These were certainly the Irish colonel and his wife of whom the landlady had spoken. They took their seats and the colonel poured out a thimbleful of wine for his wife and a thimbleful for himself. They waited in silence for their dinner to be served to them by the buxom, hearty maid.

At last the persons arrived for whom Ashenden had been waiting. He was doing his best to read a German book and it was only by an exercise of self-control that he allowed himself only for one instant to raise his eyes as they came in. His glance showed him a man of about forty-five with short dark hair, somewhat grizzled, of middle height, but corpulent, with a broad red clean-shaven face. He wore a shirt open at the neck, with a wide collar, and a grey suit. He walked ahead of his wife, and of her Ashenden only caught the impression of a German woman self-effaced and dusty. Grantley Caypor sat down and began in a loud voice explaining to the waitress that they had taken an immense walk. They had been up some mountain the name of which meant nothing to Ashenden, but which excited in the maid expressions of astonishment and enthusiasm. Then Caypor, still in fluent German but with a marked English accent, said that they were so late they had not even gone up to wash, but had just rinsed their hands outside. He had a resonant voice and a jovial manner.

'Serve me quick, we're starving with hunger, and bring beer, bring three bottles. *Lieber Gott*, what a thirst I have!'

He seemed to be a man of exuberant vitality. He brought into that dull, overclean dining-room the breath of life and everyone in it appeared on a sudden more alert. He began to talk to his wife, in English, and everything he said could be heard by all; but presently she interrupted him with a remark made in an undertone. Caypor stopped and Ashenden felt that his eyes were turned in his direction. Mrs Caypor had noticed the arrival of a stranger and had drawn her husband's attention to it. Ashenden turned the page of the book he was pretending to read, but he felt that Caypor's gaze was fixed intently upon him. When he addressed his wife again it was in so low a tone that Ashenden could not even tell what language he used, but when the maid brought them their soup Caypor, his voice still low, asked her a question. It was plain that he was enquiring who Ashenden was. Ashenden could catch of the maid's reply but the one word *länder*.

One or two people finished their dinner and went out picking their teeth. The old Irish colonel and his old wife rose from their table and he stood aside to let her pass. They had eaten their meal without exchanging a word. She walked slowly to the door; but the colonel stopped to say a word to a Swiss who might have been a local attorney, and when she reached it she stood there, bowed and with a sheep-like look, patiently waiting for her husband to come and open it for her. Ashenden realized that she had never opened a door for herself. She did not know how to. In a minute the colonel with his old, old gait came to the door and opened it; she passed out and he followed. The little incident offered a key to their whole lives, and from it Ashenden began to reconstruct their histories, circumstances and characters; but he pulled himself up; he could not allow himself the luxury of creation. He finished his dinner.

When he went into the hall he saw tied to the leg of a table a bull-terrier and in passing mechanically put down his hand to fondle the dog's drooping, soft ears. The landlady was standing at the foot of the stairs.

'Whose is this lovely beast?' asked Ashenden.

'He belongs to Herr Caypor. Fritzi, he is called. Herr Caypor says he has a longer pedigree than the King of England.'

Fritzi rubbed himself against Ashenden's leg and with his nose sought the palm of his hand. Ashenden went upstairs to fetch his hat, and when he came down saw Caypor standing at the entrance of the hotel talking with the landlady. From the sudden silence and their constrained manner he guessed that Caypor had been making enquiries about him. When he passed between them, into the street, out of the corner of his eye he saw Caypor give a suspicious stare. That frank, jovial red face bore then a look of shifty cunning.

Ashenden strolled along till he found a tavern where he could have his coffee in the open and to compensate himself for the bottle of beer that his sense of duty had urged him to drink at dinner ordered the best brandy the house provided. He was pleased at last to have come face to face with the man of whom he had heard so much and in a day or two hoped to become acquainted with him. It is never very difficult to get to know anyone who has a dog. But he was in no hurry; he would let things take their course: with the object he had in view he could not afford to be hasty.

Ashenden reviewed the circumstances. Grantley Caypor was an Englishman, born according to his passport in Birmingham, and he was forty-two years of age. His wife, to whom he had been married for eleven years, was of German birth and parentage. That was public knowledge. Information about his antecedents was contained in a private document. He had started life, according to this, in a lawyer's office in Birmingham and then had drifted into journalism. He had been connected with an English paper in Cairo and with another in Shanghai. There he got into trouble for attempting to get money on false pretences and was sentenced to a short term of imprisonment. All trace of him was lost for two years after his release, when he reappeared in a shipping-office in Marseilles. From there, still in the shipping business, he went to Hamburg, where he married, and to London. In London he set up for himself in the export business, but after some time failed and was made a bankrupt. He returned to journalism. At the outbreak of war he was once more in the shipping business, and in August, 1914, was living quietly with his German wife at Southampton. In the beginning of the following year he told his employers that owing to the nationality of his wife his position was intolerable; they had no fault to find with him and, recognizing that he was in an awkward fix, granted his request that he should be transferred to Genoa. Here he remained till Italy entered the war, but then gave notice and with his papers in perfect order crossed the border and took up his residence in Switzerland.

All this indicated a man of doubtful honesty and unsettled disposition, with no background and of no financial standing; but the facts were of no importance to anyone till it was discovered that Caypor, certainly from the beginning of the war and perhaps sooner, was in the service of the German Intelligence Department. He had a salary of forty pounds a month. But though dangerous and wily no steps would have been taken to deal with him if he had contented himself with transmitting such news as he was able to get in Switzerland. He could do no great harm there and it might even be possible to make use of him to convey information that it was desirable to let the enemy have. He had no notion that anything was known of him. His letters, and he received a good many, were closely censored; there were few codes that the people who dealt with such matters could not in the end decipher and it might be that sooner or later through him it would be possible to lay hands on the organization that still flourished in England. But then he did something that drew R.'s attention to him. Had he known it none could have blamed him for shaking in his shoes: R. was not a very nice man to get on the wrong side of. Caypor scraped acquaintance in Zurich with a young Spaniard, Gomez by name, who had lately entered the British Secret Service, by his nationality inspired him with confidence, and managed to worm out of him the fact that he was engaged in espionage. Probably the Spaniard, with a very human desire to seem important, had done no more than talk mysteriously; but on Caypor's information he was watched when he went to Germany and one day caught just as he was posting a letter in a code that was eventually deciphered. He was tried, convicted and shot. It was bad enough to lose a useful and disinterested agent, but it entailed besides the changing of a safe and simple code. R. was not pleased. But R. was not the man to let any desire of revenge stand in the way of his main object, and it occurred to him that if Caypor was merely betraying his country for money it might be possible to get him to take more money to betray his employers. The fact that he had succeeded in delivering into their hands an agent of the Allies must seem to them an earnest of his good faith. He might be very useful. But R. had no notion what kind of man Caypor was, he had lived his shabby, furtive life obscurely, and the only photograph that existed of him was one taken for a passport. Ashenden's instructions were to get acquainted with Caypor and see whether there was any chance that he would work honestly for the British: if he thought there was, he was entitled to sound him and if his suggestions were met with favour to make certain propositions. It was a task that needed tact and a knowledge of men. If on the other hand Ashenden came to the conclusion that Caypor could not be bought, he was to watch and report his movements. The information he had obtained from Gustav was vague, but important; there was only one point in it that was interesting, and this was that the head of the German Intelligence Department in Berne was growing restive at Caypor's lack of activity. Caypor was asking for a higher salary and Major von P. had told him that he must earn it. It might be that he was urging him to go to England. If he could be induced to cross the frontier Ashenden's work was done.

'How the devil do you expect *me* to persuade him to put his head in a noose?' asked Ashenden.

'It won't be a noose, it'll be a firing-squad,' said R.

'Caypor's clever.'

'Well, be cleverer, damn your eyes.'

Ashenden made up his mind that he would take no steps to make Caypor's acquaintance, but allow the first advances to be made by him. If he was being pressed for results it must surely occur to him that it would be worth while to get into conversation with an Englishman who was employed in the Censorship

Department. Ashenden was prepared with a supply of information that it could not in the least benefit the Central Powers to possess. With a false name and a false passport he had little fear that Caypor would guess that he was a British agent.

Ashenden did not have to wait long. Next day he was sitting in the doorway of the hotel, drinking a cup of coffee and already half asleep after a substantial *mittagessen*, when the Caypors came out of the dining-room. Mrs Caypor went upstairs and Caypor released his dog. The dog bounded along and in a friendly fashion leaped up against Ashenden.

'Come here, Fritzi,' cried Caypor, and then to Ashenden: 'I'm so sorry. But he's quite gentle.'

'Oh, that's all right. He won't hurt me.'

Caypor stopped at the doorway.

'He's a bull-terrier. You don't often see them on the Continent.' He seemed while he spoke to be taking Ashenden's measure; he called to the maid: 'A coffee, please, *fräulein*. You've just arrived, haven't you?'

'Yes, I came yesterday.'

'Really? I didn't see you in the dining-room last night. Are you making a stay?'

'I don't know. I've been ill and I've come here to recuperate.'

The maid came with the coffee and seeing Caypor talking to Ashenden put the tray on the table at which he was sitting. Caypor gave a laugh of faint embarrassment.

'I don't want to force myself upon you. I don't know why the maid put my coffee on your table.'

'Please sit down,' said Ashenden.

'It's very good of you. I've lived so long on the Continent that I'm always forgetting that my countrymen are apt to look upon it as confounded cheek if you talk to them. Are you English, by the way, or American?'

'English,' said Ashenden.

Ashenden was by nature a very shy person, and he had in vain

C

tried to cure himself of a failing that at his age was unseemly, but on occasion he knew how to make effective use of it. He explained now in a hesitating and awkward manner the facts that he had the day before told the landlady and that he was convinced she had already passed on to Caypor.

'You couldn't have come to a better place than Lucerne. It's an oasis of peace in this war-weary world. When you're here you might almost forget that there is such a thing as a war going on. That is why I've come here. I'm a journalist by profession.'

'I couldn't help wondering if you wrote,' said Ashenden, with an eagerly timid smile.

It was clear that he had not learnt that 'oasis of peace in a war-weary world' at the shipping-office.

'You see, I married a German lady,' said Caypor gravely.

'Oh, really?'

'I don't think anyone could be more patriotic than I am. I'm English through and through and I don't mind telling you that in my opinion the British Empire is the greatest instrument for good that the world has ever seen, but having a German wife I naturally see a good deal of the reverse of the medal. You don't have to tell me that the Germans have faults, but frankly I'm not prepared to admit that they're devils incarnate. At the beginning of the war my poor wife had a very rough time in England and I for one couldn't have blamed her if she'd felt rather bitter about it. Everyone thought she was a spy. It'll make you laugh when you know her. She's the typical German *hausfrau* who cares for nothing but her house and her husband and our only child Fritzi.' Caypor fondled his dog and gave a little laugh. 'Yes, Fritzi, you are our child, aren't you? Naturally it made my position very awkward. I was connected with some very important papers, and my editors weren't quite comfortable about it. Well, to cut a long story short, I thought the most dignified course was to resign and come to a neutral country till the storm blew over. My wife and I never discuss the war, though

I'm bound to tell you that it's more on my account than hers, she's much more tolerant than I am and she's more willing to look upon this terrible business from my point of view than I am from hers.'

'That is strange,' said Ashenden. 'As a rule women are so much more rabid than men.'

'My wife is a very remarkable person. I should like to introduce you to her. By the way, I don't know if you know my name. Grantley Caypor.'

'My name is Somerville,' said Ashenden.

He told him then of the work he had been doing in the Censorship Department, and he fancied that into Caypor's eyes came a certain intentness. Presently he told him that he was looking for someone to give him conversation lessons in German so that he might rub up his rusty knowledge of the language; and as he spoke a notion flashed across his mind: he gave Caypor a look and saw that the same notion had come to him. It had occurred to them at the same instant that it would be a very good plan for Ashenden's teacher to be Mrs Caypor.

'I asked our landlady if she could find me someone and she said she thought she could. I must ask her again. It ought not to be very hard to find a man who is prepared to come and talk German to me for an hour a day.'

'I wouldn't take anyone on the landlady's recommendation,' said Caypor. 'After all you want someone with a good North-German accent and she only talks Swiss. I'll ask my wife if she knows anyone. My wife's a very highly educated woman and you could trust her recommendation.'

'That's very kind of you.'

Ashenden observed Grantley Caypor at his ease. He noticed how the small, grey-green eyes, which last night he had not been able to see, contradicted the red good-humoured frankness of the face. They were quick and shifty, but when the mind behind them was seized by an unexpected notion they were suddenly still. It gave one a peculiar feeling of the working of the brain. They were not eyes that inspired confidence; Caypor did that with his jolly, good-natured smile, the openness of his broad, weather-beaten face, his comfortable obesity and the cheeriness of his loud, deep voice. He was doing his best now to be agreeable. While Ashenden talked to him, a little shyly still but gaining confidence from that breezy, cordial manner, capable of putting anyone at his ease, it intrigued him to remember that the man was a common spy. It gave a tang to his conversation to reflect that he had been ready to sell his country for no more than forty pounds a month. Ashenden had known Gomez, the young Spaniard whom Caypor had betrayed. He was a high-spirited youth, with a love of adventure, and he had undertaken his dangerous mission not for the money he earned by it, but from a passion for romance. It amused him to outwit the clumsy German and it appealed to his sense of the absurd to play a part in a shilling shocker. It was not very nice to think of him now six feet underground in a prison yard. He was young and he had a certain grace of gesture. Ashenden wondered whether Caypor had felt a qualm when he delivered him up to destruction.

'I suppose you know a little German?' asked Caypor, interested in the stranger.

'Oh, yes, I was a student in Germany, and I used to talk it fluently, but that is long ago and I have forgotten. I can still read it very comfortably.'

'Oh, yes, I noticed you were reading a German book last night.'

Fool! It was only a little while since he had told Ashenden that he had not seen him at dinner. He wondered whether Caypor had observed the slip. How difficult it was never to make one! Ashenden must be on his guard; the thing that made him most nervous was the thought that he might not answer readily enough to his assumed name of Somerville. Of course there was always the chance that Caypor had made the slip on purpose to see by Ashenden's face whether he noticed anything. Caypor got up.

'There is my wife. We go for a walk up one of the mountains every afternoon. I can tell you some charming walks. The flowers even now are lovely.'

'I'm afraid I must wait till I'm a bit stronger,' said Ashenden, with a little sigh.

He had naturally a pale face and never looked as robust as he was. Mrs Caypor came downstairs and her husband joined her. They walked down the road, Fritzi bounding round them, and Ashenden saw that Caypor immediately began to speak with volubility. He was evidently telling his wife the results of his interview with Ashenden. Ashenden looked at the sun shining so gaily on the lake; the shadow of a breeze fluttered the green leaves of the trees; everything invited to a stroll: he got up, went to his room and throwing himself on his bed had a very pleasant sleep.

He went into dinner that evening as the Caypors were finishing, for he had wandered melancholy about Lucerne in the hope of finding a cocktail that would enable him to face the potato salad that he foresaw, and on their way out of the dining-room Caypor stopped and asked him if he would drink coffee with them. When Ashenden joined them in the hall Caypor got up and introduced him to his wife. She bowed stiffly and no answering smile came to her face to respond to Ashenden's civil greeting. It was not hard to see that her attitude was definitely hostile. It put Ashenden at his ease. She was a plainish woman, nearing forty, with a muddy skin and vague features; her drab hair was arranged in a plait round her head like that of Napoleon's Queen of Prussia; and she was squarely built, plump rather than fat, and solid. But she did not look stupid; she looked, on the contrary, a woman of character and Ashenden, who had lived enough in Germany to recognize the type, was ready to believe that though capable of doing the housework, cooking the dinner

and climbing a mountain, she might be also prodigiously well
informed. She wore a white blouse that showed a sunburned
neck, a black skirt and heavy walking boots. Caypor addressing
her in English told her in his jovial way, as though she did not
know it already, what Ashenden had told him about himself.
She listened grimly.

'I think you told me you understood German,' said Caypor,
his big red face wreathed in polite smiles but his little eyes dart-
ing about restlessly.

'Yes, I was for some time a student in Heidelberg.'

'Really?' said Mrs Caypor in English, an expression of faint
interest for a moment chasing away the sullenness from her face.
'I know Heidelberg very well. I was at school there for one year.'

Her English was correct, but throaty, and the mouthing
emphasis she gave her words was disagreeable. Ashenden was
diffuse in praise of the old university town and the beauty of
the neighbourhood. She heard him, from the standpoint of
her Teutonic superiority, with toleration rather than with
enthusiasm.

'It is well known that the valley of the Neckar is one of the
beauty places of the whole world,' she said.

'I have not told you, my dear,' said Caypor then, 'that Mr
Somerville is looking for someone to give him conversation
lessons while he is here. I told him that perhaps you could
suggest a teacher.'

'No, I know no one whom I could conscientiously recom-
mend,' she answered. 'The Swiss accent is hateful beyond words.
It could do Mr Somerville only harm to converse with a Swiss.'

'If I were in your place, Mr Somerville, I would try and persuade my wife to give you lessons. She is, if I may say so, a
very cultivated and highly educated woman.'

'*Ach*, Grantley, I have not the time. I have my own work
to do.'

Ashenden saw that he was being given his opportunity. The

trap was prepared and all he had to do was to fall in. He turned
to Mrs Caypor with a manner that he tried to make shy, de-
precating and modest.

'Of course it would be too wonderful if you would give me
lessons. I should look upon it as a real privilege. Naturally I
wouldn't want to interfere with your work. I am just here to
get well, with nothing in the world to do, and I would suit my
time entirely to your convenience.'

He felt a flash of satisfaction pass from one to the other and
in Mrs Caypor's blue eyes he fancied that he saw a dark glow.

'Of course it would be a purely business arrangement,' said
Caypor. 'There's no reason that my good wife shouldn't earn a
little pin-money. Would you think ten francs an hour too much?'

'No,' said Ashenden, 'I should think myself lucky to get a
first-rate teacher for that.'

'What do you say, my dear? Surely you can spare an hour,
and you would be doing this gentleman a kindness. He would
learn that all Germans are not the devilish fiends that they think
them in England.'

On Mrs Caypor's brow was an uneasy frown and Ashenden
could not but think with apprehension of that hour's conversation a day that he was going to exchange with her. Heaven only
knew how he would have to rack his brain for subjects of dis-
course with that heavy and morose woman. Now she made a
visible effort.

'I shall be very pleased to give Mr Somerville conversation
lessons.'

'I congratulate you, Mr Somerville,' said Caypor noisily.
'You're in for a treat. When will you start, tomorrow at eleven?'

'That would suit me very well if it suits Mrs Caypor.'

'Yes, that is as good an hour as another,' she answered.

Ashenden left them to discuss the happy outcome of their
diplomacy. But when, punctually at eleven next morning, he
heard a knock at his door (for it had been arranged that Mrs

Caypor should give him his lesson in his room) it was not without trepidation that he opened it. It behoved him to be frank,
a trifle indiscreet, but obviously wary of a German woman,
sufficiently intelligent, and impulsive. Mrs Caypor's face was
dark and sulky. She plainly hated having anything to do with
him. But they sat down and she began, somewhat peremptorily,
to ask him questions about his knowledge of German literature.
She corrected his mistakes with exactness and when he put before her some difficulty in German construction explained it
with clearness and precision. It was obvious that though she
hated giving him a lesson she meant to give it conscientiously.
She seemed to have not only an aptitude for teaching, but a love
of it, and as the hour went on she began to speak with greater
earnestness. It was already only by an effort that she remembered that he was a brutal Englishman. Ashenden, noticing the
unconscious struggle within her, found himself not a little enter-
tained; and it was with truth that, when later in the day Caypor
asked him how the lesson had gone, he answered that it was
highly satisfactory; Mrs Caypor was an excellent teacher and
a most interesting person.

'I told you so. She's the most remarkable woman I know.'

And Ashenden had a feeling that when in his hearty, laughing
way Caypor said this he was for the first time entirely sincere.

In a day or two Ashenden guessed that Mrs Caypor was giving
him lessons only in order to enable Caypor to arrive at a closer
intimacy with him, for she confined herself strictly to matters
of literature, music and painting; and when Ashenden, by way
of experiment, brought the conversation round to the war, she
cut him short.

'I think that is a topic that we had better avoid, Herr Somerville,' she said.

She continued to give her lessons with the greatest thorough-
ness, and he had his money's worth, but every day she came
with the same sullen face and it was only in the interest of teach

ing that she lost for a moment her instinctive dislike of him. Ashenden exercised in turn, but in vain, all his wiles. He was ingratiating, ingenuous, humble, grateful, flattering, simple and timid. She remained coldly hostile. She was a fanatic. Her patriotism was aggressive, but disinterested, and obsessed with the notion of the superiority of all things German she loathed England with a virulent hatred because in that country she saw the chief obstacle to their diffusion. Her ideal was a German world in which the rest of the nations under a hegemony greater than that of Rome should enjoy the benefits of German science and German art and German culture. There was in the conception a magnificent impudence that appealed to Ashenden's sense of humour. She was no fool. She had read much, in several languages, and she could talk of the books she had read with good sense. She had a knowledge of modern painting and modern music that not a little impressed Ashenden. It was amusing once to hear her before luncheon play one of those silvery little pieces of Debussy; she played it disdainfully because it was French and so light, but with an angry appreciation of its grace and gaiety. When Ashenden congratulated her she shrugged her shoulders.

'The decadent music of a decadent nation,' she said. Then with powerful hands she struck the first resounding chords of a sonata by Beethoven; but she stopped. 'I cannot play, I am out of practice, and you English, what do you know of music? You have not produced a composer since Purcell!'

'What do you think of that statement?' Ashenden, smiling, asked Caypor, who was standing near.

'I confess its truth. The little I know of music my wife taught me. I wish you could hear her play when she is in practice.' He put his fat hand, with its square, stumpy fingers, on her shoulder. 'She can wring your heartstrings with pure beauty.'

'*Dummer Kerl*,' she said, in a soft voice, 'Stupid fellow,' and Ashenden saw her mouth for a moment quiver, but she quickly recovered. 'You English, you cannot paint, you cannot model, you cannot write music.'

'Some of us can at times write pleasing verses,' said Ashenden, with good-humour, for it was not his business to be put out, and, he did not know why, two lines occurring to him he said them:

'Whither, O splendid ship, thy white sails crowding,
Leaning across the bosom of the urgent West.'

'Yes,' said Mrs Caypor, with a strange gesture, 'you can write poetry. I wonder why.'

And to Ashenden's surprise she went on, in her guttural English, to recite the next two lines of the poem he had quoted.

'Come, Grantley, mittagessen is ready, let us go into the dining-room.'

They left Ashenden reflective.

Ashenden admired goodness, but was not outraged by wickedness. People sometimes thought him heartless because he was more often interested in others than attached to them, and even in the few to whom he was attached his eyes saw with equal clearness the merits and the defects. When he liked people it was not because he was blind to their faults, he did not mind their faults but accepted them with a tolerant shrug of the shoulders, or because he ascribed to them excellencies that they did not possess; and since he judged his friends with candour they never disappointed him and so he seldom lost one. He asked from none more than he could give. He was able to pursue his study of the Caypors without prejudice and without passion. Mrs Caypor seemed to him more of a piece and therefore the easier of the two to understand; she obviously detested him; though it was necessary for her to be civil to him her antipathy was strong enough to wring from her now and then an expression of rudeness; and had she been safely able to do so she would have killed him without a qualm. But in the pressure of Caypor's chubby hand on his wife's shoulder and in the fugitive trembling of her lips Ashenden had divined that this unprepossessing woman and that mean fat man were joined together by a deep and sincere love. It was touching. Ashenden assembled the observations that he had been making for the past few days and little things that he had noticed but to which he had attached no significance returned to him. It seemed to him that Mrs Caypor loved her husband because she was of a stronger character than he and because she felt his dependence on her; she loved him for his admiration of her, and you might guess that till she met him this dumpy, plain woman with her dullness, good sense and want of humour could not have much enjoyed the admiration of men; she enjoyed his heartiness and his noisy jokes, and his high spirits stirred her sluggish blood; he was a great big bouncing boy and he would never be anything else and she felt like a mother towards him; she had made him what he was, and he was her man and she was his woman, and she loved him, notwithstanding his weakness (for with her clear head she must always have been conscious of that), she loved him, *ach*, *was*, as Isolde loved Tristan. But then there was the espionage. Even Ashenden with all his tolerance for human frailty could not but feel that to betray your country for money is not a very pretty proceeding. Of course she knew of it, indeed it was probably through her that Caypor had first been approached; he would never have undertaken such work if she had not urged him to it. She loved him and she was an honest and an upright woman. By what devious means had she persuaded herself to force her husband to adopt so base and dishonourable a calling? Ashenden lost himself in a labyrinth of conjecture as he tried to piece together the actions of her mind.

Grantley Caypor was another story. There was little to admire in him, but at that moment Ashenden was not looking for an object of admiration; but there was much that was singular and much that was unexpected in that gross and vulgar fellow.

Ashenden watched with entertainment the suave manner in which the spy tried to inveigle him in his toils. It was a couple of days after his first lesson that Caypor after dinner, his wife having gone upstairs, threw himself heavily into a chair by Ashenden's side. His faithful Fritzi came up to him and put his long muzzle with its black nose on his knee.

'He has no brain,' said Caypor, 'but a heart of gold. Look at those little pink eyes. Did you ever see anything so stupid? And what an ugly face, but what incredible charm!'

'Have you had him long?' asked Ashenden.

'I got him in 1914 just before the outbreak of war. By the way, what do you think of the news today? Of course my wife and I never discuss the war. You can't think what a relief to me it is to find a fellow-countryman to whom I can open my heart.'

He handed Ashenden a cheap Swiss cigar and Ashenden, making a rueful sacrifice to duty, accepted it.

'Of course, they haven't got a chance, the Germans,' said Caypor, 'not a dog's chance. I knew they were beaten the moment we came in.'

His manner was earnest, sincere and confidential. Ashenden made a commonplace rejoinder.

'It's the greatest grief of my life that owing to my wife's nationality I was unable to do any war work. I tried to enlist the day war broke out, but they wouldn't have me on account of my age, but I don't mind telling you, if the war goes on much longer, wife or no wife, I'm going to do something. With my knowledge of languages I ought to be of some service in the Censorship Department. That's where you were, wasn't it?'

That was the mark at which he had been aiming and in answer now to his well-directed questions Ashenden gave him the information that he had already prepared. Caypor drew his chair a little nearer and dropped his voice.

'I'm sure you wouldn't tell me anything that anyone shouldn't know, but after all, these Swiss are absolutely pro-German and we don't want to give anyone the chance of overhearing.'

Then he went on another tack. He told Ashenden a number of things that were of a certain secrecy.

'I wouldn't tell this to anybody else, you know, but I have one or two friends who are in pretty influential positions, and they know they can trust me.'

Thus encouraged, Ashenden was a little more deliberately indiscreet and when they parted both had reason to be satisfied. Ashenden guessed that Caypor's typewriter would be kept busy next morning and that extremely energetic major in Berne would shortly receive a most interesting report.

One evening, going upstairs after dinner, Ashenden passed an open bathroom. He caught sight of the Caypors.

'Come in,' cried Caypor in his cordial way. 'We're washing our Fritzi.'

The bull-terrier was constantly getting himself very dirty, and it was Caypor's pride to see him clean and white. Ashenden went in. Mrs Caypor with her sleeves turned up and a large white apron was standing at one end of the bath, while Caypor, in a pair of trousers and a singlet, his fat, freckled arms bare, was soaping the wretched hound.

'We have to do it at night,' he said, 'because the Fitzgeralds use this bath and they'd have a fit if they knew we washed the dog in it. We wait till they go to bed. Come along, Fritzi, show the gentleman how beautifully you behave when you have your face scrubbed.'

The poor brute, woebegone but faintly wagging his tail to show that however foul was this operation performed on him he bore no malice to the god who did it, was standing in the middle of the bath in six inches of water. He was soaped all over and Caypor, talking the while, shampooed him with his great fat hands.

'Oh, what a beautiful dog he's going to be when he's as white as the driven snow. His master will be as proud as Punch to walk out with him and all the little lady dogs will say: Good gracious, who's that beautiful aristocratic-looking bull-terrier walking as though he owned the whole of Switzerland? Now stand still while you have your ears washed. You couldn't bear to go out into the street with dirty ears, could you? like a nasty little Swiss schoolboy. *Noblesse oblige*. Now the black nose. Oh, and all the soap is going into his little pink eyes and they'll smart.'

Mrs Caypor listened to this nonsense with a good-humoured sluggish smile on her broad, plain face, and presently gravely took a towel.

'Now he's going to have a ducking. Upsie-daisy.'

Caypor seized the dog by the forelegs and ducked him once and ducked him twice. There was a struggle, a flurry and a splashing. Caypor lifted him out of the bath.

'Now go to Mother and she'll dry you.'

Mrs Caypor sat down and taking the dog between her strong legs rubbed him till the sweat poured off her forehead. And Fritzi, a little shaken and breathless, but happy it was all over, stood, with his sweet stupid face, white and shining.

'Blood will tell,' cried Caypor exultantly. 'He knows the names of no less than sixty-four of his ancestors, and they were all nobly born.'

Ashenden was faintly troubled. He shivered a little as he walked upstairs.

Then, one Sunday, Caypor told him that he and his wife were going on an excursion and would eat their luncheon at some little mountain restaurant; and he suggested that Ashenden, each paying his share, should come with them. After three weeks at Lucerne Ashenden thought that his strength would permit him to venture the exertion. They started early, Mrs Caypor business-like in her walking boots and Tyrolese hat and alpenstock, and Caypor in stockings and plus-fours looking very British. The situation amused Ashenden and he was prepared to enjoy his day; but he meant to keep his eyes open; it was not inconceivable that the Caypors had discovered what he was and it would not do to go too near a precipice; Mrs Caypor would not hesitate to give him a push and Caypor for all his jolliness was an ugly customer. But on the face of it there was nothing to mar Ashenden's pleasure in the golden morning. The air was fragrant. Caypor was full of conversation. He told funny stories. He was gay and jovial. The sweat rolled off his great red face and he laughed at himself because he was so fat. To Ashenden's astonishment he showed a peculiar knowledge of the mountain flowers. Once he went out of the way to pick one he saw a little distance from the path and brought it back to his wife. He looked at it tenderly.

'Isn't it lovely?' he cried, and his shifty grey-green eyes for a moment were as candid as a child's. 'It's like a poem by Walter Savage Landor.'

'Botany is my husband's favourite science,' said Mrs Caypor. 'I laugh at him sometimes. He is devoted to flowers. Often when we have hardly had enough money to pay the butcher he has spent everything in his pocket to bring me a bunch of roses.'

'Qui fleurit sa maison fleurit son coeur,' said Grantley Caypor.

Ashenden had once or twice seen Caypor, coming in from a walk, offer Mrs Fitzgerald a nosegay of mountain flowers with an elephantine courtesy that was not entirely displeasing; and what he had just learned added a certain significance to the pretty little action. His passion for flowers was genuine and when he gave them to the old Irish lady he gave her something he valued. It showed a real kindness of heart. Ashenden had always thought botany a tedious science, but Caypor, talking exuberantly as they walked along, was able to impart to it life and interest. He must have given it a good deal of study.

'I've never written a book,' he said. 'There are too many books already and any desire to write I have is satisfied by the more immediately profitable and quite ephemeral composition of an article for a daily paper. But if I stay here much longer I have half a mind to write a book about the wild flowers of Switzerland. Oh, I wish you'd been here a little earlier. They were marvellous. But one wants to be a poet for that, and I'm only a poor newspaper-man.'

It was curious to observe how he was able to combine real emotion with false fact.

When they reached the inn, with its view of the mountains and the lake, it was good to see the sensual pleasure with which he poured down his throat a bottle of ice-cold beer. You could not but feel sympathy for a man who took so much delight in simple things. They lunched deliciously off scrambled eggs and mountain trout. Even Mrs Caypor was moved to an unwonted gentleness by her surroundings; the inn was in an agreeably rural spot, it looked like a picture of a Swiss chalet in a book of early nineteenth-century travels; and she treated Ashenden with something less than her usual hostility. When they arrived she had burst into loud German exclamations on the beauty of the scene, and now, softened perhaps too by food and drink, her eyes, dwelling on the grandeur before her, filled with tears. She stretched out her hand.

'It is dreadful and I am ashamed, notwithstanding this horrible and unjust war I can feel in my heart at the moment nothing but happiness and gratitude.'

Caypor took her hand and pressed it and, an unusual thing with him, addressing her in German, called her little pet names. It was absurd, but touching. Ashenden, leaving them to their emotions, strolled through the garden and sat down on a bench that had been prepared for the comfort of the tourist. The view was of course spectacular, but it captured you; it was like a piece of music that was obvious and meretricious, but for the moment shattered your self-control.

And as Ashenden lingered idly in that spot he pondered over the mystery of Grantley Caypor's treachery. If he liked strange people, he had found in him one who was strange beyond belief. It would be foolish to deny that he had amiable traits. His joviality was not assumed, he was without pretence a hearty fellow, and he had real good nature. He was always ready to do a kindness. Ashenden had often watched him with the old Irish colonel and his wife who were the only other residents of the hotel; he would listen good-humouredly to the old man's tedious stories of the Egyptian war, and he was charming with her. Now that Ashenden had arrived at terms of some familiarity with Caypor he found that he regarded him less with repulsion than with curiosity. He did not think that he had become a spy merely for the money; he was a man of modest tastes and what he had earned in a shipping-office must have sufficed to so good a manager as Mrs Caypor; and after war was declared there was no lack of remunerative work for men over the military age. It might be that he was one of those men who prefer devious ways to straight for some intricate pleasure they get in fooling their fellows; and that he had turned spy, not from hatred of the country that had imprisoned him, not even from love of his wife, but from a desire to score off the big-wigs who never even knew of his existence. It might be that it was vanity that impelled him, a feeling that his talents had not received the recognition they merited, or just a puckish, impish desire to do mischief. He was a crook. It is true that only two cases of dishonesty had been brought home to him, but if he had been caught twice it might be surmised that he had often been dishonest without being caught. What did Mrs Caypor think of this? They were so united that she must be aware of it. Did it make her ashamed, for her own uprightness surely none could doubt, or did she accept it as an inevitable kink in the man she loved? Did she do all she could to prevent it or did she close her eyes to something she could not help?

How much easier life would be if people were all black or all white and how much simpler it would be to act in regard to them! Was Caypor a good man who loved evil or a bad man who loved good? And how could such unreconcilable elements exist side by side and in harmony within the same heart? For one thing was clear, Caypor was disturbed by no gnawing of conscience; he did his mean and despicable work with gusto. He was a traitor who enjoyed his treachery. Though Ashenden had been studying human nature more or less consciously all his life, it seemed to him that he knew as little about it now in middle age as he had done when he was a child. Of course R. would have said to him: Why the devil do you waste your time with such nonsense? The man's a dangerous spy and your business is to lay him by the heels.

That was true enough. Ashenden had decided that it would be useless to attempt to make any arrangement with Caypor. Though doubtless he would have no feeling about betraying his employers he could certainly not be trusted. His wife's influence was too strong. Besides, notwithstanding what he had from time to time told Ashenden, he was in his heart convinced that the Central Powers must win the war, and he meant to be on the winning side. Well, then Caypor must be laid by the heels, but how he was to effect that Ashenden had no notion. Suddenly he heard a voice.

'There you are. We've been wondering where you had hidden yourself.'

He looked round and saw the Caypors strolling towards him. They were walking hand in hand.

'So this is what has kept you so quiet,' said Caypor as his eyes fell on the view. 'What a spot!'

Mrs Caypor clasped her hands.

'*Ach Gott, wie schön!*' she cried. '*Wie schön.* When I look at that blue lake and those snowy mountains I feel inclined, like Goethe's Faust, to cry to the passing moment: Tarry.'

'This is better than being in England with the excursions and alarums of war, isn't it?' said Caypor.

'Much,' said Ashenden.

'By the way, did you have any difficulty in getting out?'

'No, not the smallest.'

'I'm told they make rather a nuisance of themselves at the frontier nowadays.'

'I came through without the smallest difficulty. I don't fancy they bother much about the English. I thought the examination of passports was quite perfunctory.'

A fleeting glance passed between Caypor and his wife. Ashenden wondered what it meant. It would be strange if Caypor's thoughts were occupied with the chances of a journey to England at the very moment when he was himself reflecting on its possibility. In a little while Mrs Caypor suggested that they had better be starting back and they wandered together in the shade of trees down the mountain paths.

Ashenden was watchful. He could do nothing (and his inactivity irked him) but wait with his eyes open to seize the opportunity that might present itself. A couple of days later an incident occurred that made him certain something was in the wind. In the course of his morning lesson Mrs Caypor remarked:

'My husband has gone to Geneva today. He had some business to do there.'

'Oh,' said Ashenden, 'will he be gone long?'

'No, only two days.'

It is not everyone who can tell a lie and Ashenden had the feeling, he hardly knew why, that Mrs Caypor was telling one then. Her manner perhaps was not quite as indifferent as you would have expected when she was mentioning a fact that could be of no interest to Ashenden. It flashed across his mind that Caypor had been summoned to Berne to see the redoubtable head of the German Secret Service. When he had the chance he said casually to the waitress:

'A little less work for you to do, *fräulein*. I hear that Herr Caypor has gone to Berne.'

'Yes. But he'll be back tomorrow.'

That proved nothing, but it was something to go upon. Ashenden knew in Lucerne a Swiss who was willing on emergency to do odd jobs and, looking him up, asked him to take a letter to Berne. It might be possible to pick up Caypor and trace his movements. Next day Caypor appeared once more with his wife at the dinner-table, but merely nodded to Ashenden and afterwards both went straight upstairs. They looked troubled. Caypor, as a rule so animated, walked with bowed shoulders and looked neither to the right nor to the left. Next morning Ashenden received a reply to his letter: Caypor had seen Major von P. It was possible to guess what the major had said to him. Ashenden well knew how rough he could be; he was a hard man and brutal, clever and unscrupulous, and he was not accustomed to mince his words. They were tired of paying Caypor a salary to sit still in Lucerne and do nothing; the time was come for him to go to England. Guess-work? Of course it was guess-work, but in that trade it mostly was; you had to deduce the animal from its jawbone. Ashenden knew from Gustav that the Germans wanted to send someone to England. He drew a long breath; if Caypor went he would have to get busy.

When Mrs Caypor came in to give him his lesson she was dull and listless. She looked tired and her mouth was set obstinately. It occurred to Ashenden that the Caypors had spent most of the night talking. He wished he knew what they had said. Did she urge him to go or did she try to dissuade him? Ashenden watched them again at luncheon. Something was the matter, for they hardly spoke to one another and as a rule they found plenty to talk about. They left the room early, but when Ashenden went out he saw Caypor sitting in the hall by himself.

'Hulloa,' he cried jovially, but surely the effort was patent, 'how are you getting on? I've been to Geneva.'

'So I heard,' said Ashenden.

'Come and have your coffee with me. My poor wife's got a headache. I told her she'd better go and lie down.' In his shifty green eyes was an expression that Ashenden could not read. 'The fact is, she's rather worried, poor dear; I'm thinking of going to England.'

Ashenden's heart gave a sudden leap against his ribs, but his face remained impassive:

'Oh, are you going for long? We shall miss you.'

'To tell you the truth, I'm fed up with doing nothing. The war looks as though it were going on for years and I can't sit here indefinitely. Besides, I can't afford it, I've got to earn my living. I may have a German wife, but I am an Englishman, hang it all, and I want to do my bit. I could never face my friends again if I just stayed here in ease and comfort till the end of the war and never attempted to do a thing to help the country. My wife takes her German point of view and I don't mind telling you that she's a bit upset. You know what women are.'

Now Ashenden knew what it was that he saw in Caypor's eyes. Fear. It gave him a nasty turn. Caypor didn't want to go to England, he wanted to stay safely in Switzerland; Ashenden knew now what the major had said to him when he went to see him in Berne. He had got to go or lose his salary. What was it that his wife had said when he told her what had happened? He had wanted her to press him to stay, but, it was plain, she hadn't done that; perhaps he had not dared tell her how frightened he was; to her he had always been gay, bold, adventurous and devil-may-care; and now, the prisoner of his own lies, he had not found it in him to confess himself the mean and sneaking coward he was.

'Are you going to take your wife with you?' asked Ashenden.

'No, she'll stay here.'

It had been arranged very neatly. Mrs Caypor would receive his letters and forward the information they contained to Berne.

'I've been out of England so long that I don't quite know how to set about getting war work. What would you do in my place?'

'I don't know; what sort of work are you thinking of?'

'Well, you know, I imagine I could do the same thing as you did. I wonder if there's anyone in the Censorship Department that you could give me a letter of introduction to.'

It was only by a miracle that Ashenden saved himself from showing by a smothered cry or by a broken gesture how startled he was; but not by Caypor's request, by what had just dawned upon him. What an idiot he had been! He had been disturbed by the thought that he was wasting his time at Lucerne, he was doing nothing, and though in fact, as it turned out, Caypor was going to England it was due to no cleverness of his. He could take to himself no credit for the result. And now he saw that he had been put in Lucerne, told how to describe himself and given the proper information, so that what actually had occurred should occur. It would be a wonderful thing for the German Secret Service to get an agent into the Censorship Department; and by a happy accident there was Grantley Caypor, the very man for the job, on friendly terms with someone who had worked there. What a bit of luck! Major von P. was a man of culture and, rubbing his hands, he must surely have murmured: *stultum facit fortuna quem vult perdere.* It was a trap of that devilish R. and the grim major at Berne had fallen into it. Ashenden had done his work just by sitting still and doing nothing. He almost laughed as he thought what a fool R. had made of him.

'I was on very good terms with the chief of my department, I could give you a note to him if you liked.'

'That would be just the thing.'

'But of course I must give the facts. I must say I've met you here and only known you a fortnight.'

'Of course. But you'll say what else you can for me, won't you?'

'Oh, certainly.'

'I don't know yet if I can get a visa. I'm told they're rather fussy.'

'I don't see why. I shall be very sick if they refuse me one when I want to go back.'

'I'll go and see how my wife is getting on,' said Caypor suddenly, getting up. 'When will you let me have that letter?'

'Whenever you like. Are you going at once?'

'As soon as possible.'

Caypor left him. Ashenden waited in the hall for a quarter of an hour so that there should appear in him no sign of hurry. Then he went upstairs and prepared various communications. In one he informed R. that Caypor was going to England; in another he made arrangements through Berne that wherever Caypor applied for a visa it should be granted to him without question; and these he despatched forthwith. When he went down to dinner he handed Caypor a cordial letter of introduction.

Next day but one Caypor left Lucerne.

Ashenden waited. He continued to have his hour's lesson with Mrs Caypor and under her conscientious tuition began now to speak German with ease. They talked of Goethe and Winckelmann, of art and life and travel. Fritzi sat quietly by her chair.

'He misses his master,' she said, pulling his ears. 'He only really cares for him, he suffers me only as belonging to him.'

After his lesson Ashenden went every morning to Cook's to ask for his letters. It was here that all communications were addressed to him. He could not move till he received instructions, but R. could be trusted not to leave him idle long; and meanwhile there was nothing for him to do but have patience. Presently he received a letter from the consul in Geneva to say that Caypor had there applied for his visa and had set out for France. Having read this Ashenden went on for a little stroll by the lake and on his way back happened to see Mrs Caypor coming out of Cook's office. He guessed that she was having her letters addressed there too. He went up to her.

'Have you had news of Herr Caypor?' he asked her.

'No,' she said. 'I suppose I could hardly expect to yet.'

He walked along by her side. She was disappointed, but not yet anxious; she knew how irregular at that time was the post. But next day during the lesson he could not but see that she was impatient to have done with it. The post was delivered at noon and at five minutes to she looked at her watch and him. Though Ashenden knew very well that no letter would ever come for her he had not the heart to keep her on tenterhooks.

'Don't you think that's enough for the day? I'm sure you want to go down to Cook's,' he said.

'Thank you. That is very amiable of you.'

When a little later he went there himself he found her standing in the middle of the office. Her face was distraught. She addressed him wildly.

'My husband promised to write from Paris. I am sure there is a letter for me, but these stupid people say there's nothing. They're so careless, it's a scandal.'

Ashenden did not know what to say. While the clerk was looking through the bundle to see if there was anything for him she came up to the desk again.

'When does the next post come in from France?' she asked.

'Sometimes there are letters about five.'

'I'll come then.'

She turned and walked rapidly away. Fritzi followed her with his tail between his legs. There was no doubt of it, already the fear had seized her that something was wrong. Next morning she looked dreadful; she could not have closed her eyes all night; and in the middle of the lesson she started up from her chair.

'You must excuse me, Herr Somerville, I cannot give you a lesson today. I am not feeling well.'

Before Ashenden could say anything she had flung nervously

from the room, and in the evening he got a note from her to say that she regretted that she must discontinue giving him conversation lessons. She gave no reason. Then Ashenden saw no more of her; she ceased coming in to meals; except to go morning and afternoon to Cook's she spent apparently the whole day in her room. Ashenden thought of her sitting there hour after hour with that hideous fear gnawing at her heart. Who could help feeling sorry for her? The time hung heavy on his hands too. He read a good deal and wrote a little, he hired a canoe and went for long leisurely paddles on the lake; and at last one morning the clerk at Cook's handed him a letter. It was from R. It had all the appearance of a business communication, but between the lines he read a good deal.

Dear Sir, it began, *The goods, with accompanying letter, despatched by you from Lucerne have been duly delivered. We are obliged to you for executing our instructions with such promptness.*

It went on in this strain. R. was exultant. Ashenden guessed that Caypor had been arrested and by now had paid the penalty of his crime. He shuddered. He remembered a dreadful scene. Dawn. A cold, grey dawn, with a drizzling rain falling. A man, blindfolded, standing against a wall, an officer very pale giving an order, a volley, and then a young soldier, one of the firing-party, turning round and holding on to his gun for support, vomiting. The officer turning paler still, and he, Ashenden, feeling dreadfully faint. How terrified Caypor must have been! It was awful when the tears ran down their faces. Ashenden shook himself. He went to the ticket-office and obedient to his orders bought himself a ticket for Geneva.

As he was waiting for his change Mrs Caypor came in. He was shocked at the sight of her. She was blowsy and dishevelled and there were heavy rings round her eyes. She was deathly pale. She staggered up to the desk and asked for a letter. The clerk shook his head.

'I'm sorry, madam, there's nothing yet.'

'But look, look. Are you sure? Please look again.'

The misery in her voice was heartrending. The clerk with a shrug of the shoulders took out the letters from a pigeon-hole and sorted them once more.

'No, there's nothing, madam.'

She gave a hoarse cry of despair and her face was distorted with anguish.

'Oh, God, oh, God,' she moaned.

She turned away, the tears streaming from her weary eyes, and for a moment she stood there like a blind man groping and not knowing which way to go. Then a fearful thing happened, Fritzi, the bull-terrier, sat down on his haunches and threw back his head and gave a long, long melancholy howl. Mrs Caypor looked at him with terror; her eyes seemed really to start from her head. The doubt, the gnawing doubt that had tortured her during those dreadful days of suspense, was a doubt no longer. She knew. She staggered blindly into the street.

The Verger

THERE had been a christening that afternoon at St Peter's, Neville Square, and Albert Edward Foreman still wore his verger's gown. He kept his new one, its folds as full and stiff as though it were made not of alpaca but of perennial bronze, for funerals and weddings (St Peter's, Neville Square, was a church much favoured by the fashionable for these ceremonies) and now he wore only his second-best. He wore it with complacence, for it was the dignified symbol of his office, and without it (when he took it off to go home) he had the disconcerting sensation of being somewhat insufficiently clad. He took pains with it; he pressed it and ironed it himself. During the sixteen years he had been verger of this church he had had a succession of such gowns, but he had never been able to throw them away when they were worn out and the complete series, neatly wrapped up in brown paper, lay in the bottom drawers of the wardrobe in his bedroom.

The verger busied himself quietly, replacing the painted wooden cover on the marble font, taking away a chair that had been brought for an infirm old lady, and waited for the vicar to have finished in the vestry so that he could tidy up in there and go home. Presently he saw him walk across the chancel, genuflect in front of the high altar and come down the aisle; but he still wore his cassock.

'What's he 'anging about for?' the verger said to himself. 'Don't 'e know I want my tea?'

The vicar had been but recently appointed, a red-faced

energetic man in the early forties, and Albert Edward still regretted his predecessor, a clergyman of the old school who preached leisurely sermons in a silvery voice and dined out a great deal with his more aristocratic parishioners. He liked things in church to be just so, but he never fussed; he was not like this new man who wanted to have his finger in every pie. But Albert Edward was tolerant. St Peter's was in a very good neighbourhood and the parishioners were a very nice class of people. The new vicar had come from the East End and he couldn't be expected to fall in all at once with the discreet ways of his fashionable congregation.

'All this 'ustle,' said Albert Edward. 'But give 'im time, he'll learn.'

When the vicar had walked down the aisle so far that he could address the verger without raising his voice more than was becoming in a place of worship he stopped.

'Foreman, will you come into the vestry for a minute. I have something to say to you.'

'Very good, sir.'

The vicar waited for him to come up and they walked up the church together.

'A very nice christening, I thought, sir. Funny 'ow the baby stopped cryin' the moment you took him.'

'I've noticed they very often do,' said the vicar, with a little smile. 'After all I've had a good deal of practice with them.'

It was a source of subdued pride to him that he could nearly always quiet a whimpering infant by the manner in which he held it and he was not unconscious of the amused admiration with which mothers and nurses watched him settle the baby in the crook of his surpliced arm. The verger knew that it pleased him to be complimented on his talent.

The vicar preceded Albert Edward into the vestry. Albert Edward was a trifle surprised to find the two churchwardens there. He had not seen them come in. They gave him pleasant nods.

'Good-afternoon, my lord. Good-afternoon, sir,' he said to one after the other.

They were elderly men, both of them, and they had been churchwardens almost as long as Albert Edward had been verger. They were sitting now at a handsome refectory table that the old vicar had brought many years before from Italy and the vicar sat down in the vacant chair between them. Albert Edward faced them, the table between him and them, and wondered with slight uneasiness what was the matter. He remembered still the occasion on which the organist had got into trouble and the bother they had all had to hush things up. In a church like St Peter's, Neville Square, they couldn't afford a scandal. On the vicar's red face was a look of resolute benignity, but the others bore an expression that was slightly troubled.

'He's been naggin' them, he 'as,' said the verger to himself. 'He's jockeyed them into doin' something, but they don't 'alf like it. That's what it is, you mark my words.'

But his thoughts did not appear on Albert Edward's clean-cut and distinguished features. He stood in a respectful but not obsequious attitude. He had been in service before he was appointed to his ecclesiastical office, but only in very good houses, and his deportment was irreproachable. Starting as a page-boy in the household of a merchant prince, he had risen by due degrees from the position of fourth to first footman, for a year he had been single-handed butler to a widowed peeress and, till the vacancy occurred at St Peter's, butler with two men under him in the house of a retired ambassador. He was tall, spare, grave and dignified. He looked, if not like a duke, at least like an actor of the old school who specialized in dukes' parts. He had tact, firmness and self-assurance. His character was un-impeachable.

The vicar began briskly.

'Foreman, we've got something rather unpleasant to say to you. You've been here a great many years and I think his lordship and the general agree with me that you've fulfilled the duties of your office to the satisfaction of everybody concerned.'

The two churchwardens nodded.

'But a most extraordinary circumstance came to my knowledge the other day and I felt it my duty to impart it to the churchwardens. I discovered to my astonishment that you could neither read nor write.'

The verger's face betrayed no sign of embarrassment.

'The last vicar knew that, sir,' he replied. 'He said it didn't make no difference. He always said there was a great deal too much education in the world for 'is taste.'

'It's the most amazing thing I ever heard,' cried the general. 'Do you mean to say that you've been verger of this church for sixteen years and never learned to read or write?'

'I went into service when I was twelve, sir. The cook in the first place tried to teach me once, but I didn't seem to 'ave the knack for it, and then what with one thing and another I never seemed to 'ave the time. I've never really found the want of it. I think a lot of these young fellows waste a rare lot of time readin' when they might be doin' something useful.'

'But don't you want to know the news?' said the other churchwarden. 'Don't you ever want to write a letter?'

'No, me lord, I seem to manage very well without. And of late years now they've all these pictures in the papers I get to know what's goin' on pretty well. Me wife's quite a scholar and if I want to write a letter she writes it for me. It's not as if I was a bettin' man.'

The two churchwardens gave the vicar a troubled glance and then looked down at the table.

'Well, Foreman, I've talked the matter over with these gentlemen and they quite agree with me that the situation is impossible. At a church like St Peter's, Neville Square, we cannot have a verger who can neither read nor write.'

Albert Edward's thin, sallow face reddened and he moved uneasily on his feet, but he made no reply.

'Understand me, Foreman, I have no complaint to make against you. You do your work quite satisfactorily; I have the highest opinion both of your character and of your capacity; but we haven't the right to take the risk of some accident that might happen owing to your lamentable ignorance. It's a matter of prudence as well as of principle.'

'But couldn't you learn, Foreman?' asked the general.

'No, sir, I'm afraid I couldn't, not now. You see, I'm not as young as I was and if I couldn't seem able to get the letters in me 'ead when I was a nipper I don't think there's much chance of it now.'

'We don't want to be harsh with you, Foreman,' said the vicar. 'But the churchwardens and I have quite made up our minds. We'll give you three months and if at the end of that time you cannot read and write I'm afraid you'll have to go.'

Albert Edward had never liked the new vicar. He'd said from the beginning that they'd made a mistake when they gave him St Peter's. He wasn't the type of man they wanted with a classy congregation like that. And now he straightened himself a little. He knew his value and he wasn't going to allow himself to be put upon.

'I'm very sorry, sir, I'm afraid it's no good. I'm too old a dog to learn new tricks. I've lived a good many years without knowin' 'ow to read and write, and without wishin' to praise myself, self-praise is no recommendation, I don't mind sayin' I've done my duty in that state of life in which it 'as pleased a merciful providence to place me, and if I *could* learn now I don't know as I'd want to.'

'In that case, Foreman, I'm afraid you must go.'

'Yes, sir, I quite understand. I shall be 'appy to 'and in my resignation as soon as you've found somebody to take my place.'

But when Albert Edward with his usual politeness had closed the church door behind the vicar and the two churchwardens he could not sustain the air of unruffled dignity with which he had borne the blow inflicted upon him and his lips quivered. He walked slowly back to the vestry and hung up on its proper peg his verger's gown. He sighed as he thought of all the grand funerals and smart weddings it had seen. He tidied everything up, put on his coat, and hat in hand walked down the aisle. He locked the church door behind him. He strolled across the square, but deep in his sad thoughts he did not take the street that led him home, where a nice strong cup of tea awaited him; he took the wrong turning. He walked slowly along. His heart was heavy. He did not know what he should do with himself. He did not fancy the notion of going back to domestic service; after being his own master for so many years, for the vicar and churchwardens could say what they liked, it was he that had run St Peter's, Neville Square, he could scarcely demean himself by accepting a situation. He had saved a tidy sum, but not enough to live on without doing something, and life seemed to cost more every year. He had never thought to be troubled with such questions. The vergers of St Peter's, like the popes of Rome, were there for life. He had often thought of the pleasant reference the vicar would make in his sermon at evensong the first Sunday after his death to the long and faithful service, and the exemplary character of their late verger, Albert Edward Foreman. He sighed deeply. Albert Edward was a non-smoker and a total abstainer, but with a certain latitude; that is to say he liked a glass of beer with his dinner and when he was tired he enjoyed a cigarette. It occurred to him now that one would comfort him and since he did not carry them he looked about him for a shop where he could buy a packet of Gold Flakes. He did not at once see one and walked on a little. It was a long

treet, with all sorts of shops in it, but there was not a single
one where you could buy cigarettes.

'That's strange,' said Albert Edward.

To make sure he walked right up the street again. No, there
was no doubt about it. He stopped and looked reflectively up
and down.

'I can't be the only man as walks along this street and wants
a fag,' he said. 'I shouldn't wonder but what a fellow might
do very well with a little shop here. Tobacco and sweets, you
know.'

He gave a sudden start.

'That's an idea,' he said. 'Strange 'ow things come to you
when you least expect it.'

He turned, walked home, and had his tea.

'You're very silent this afternoon, Albert,' his wife remarked.

'I'm thinkin',' he said.

He considered the matter from every point of view and next
day he went along the street and by good luck found a little
shop to let that looked as though it would exactly suit him.
Twenty-four hours later he had taken it and when a month
after that he left St Peter's, Neville Square, for ever, Albert
Edward Foreman set up in business as a tobacconist and news-
agent. His wife said it was a dreadful come-down after being
verger of St Peter's, but he answered that you had to move
with the times, the church wasn't what it was, and 'ence
forward he was going to render unto Cæsar what was Cæsar's.
Albert Edward did very well. He did so well that in a year or
so it struck him that he might take a second shop and put a
manager in. He looked for another long street that hadn't got
a tobacconist in it and when he found it, and a shop to let, took
it and stocked it. This was a success too. Then it occurred to
him that if he could run two he could run half a dozen, so he
began walking about London, and whenever he found a long
street that had no tobacconist and a shop to let he took it. In

the course of ten years he had acquired no less than ten shops and he was making money hand over fist. He went round to all of them himself every Monday, collected the week's takings and took them to the bank.

One morning when he was there paying in a bundle of notes and a heavy bag of silver the cashier told him that the manager would like to see him. He was shown into an office and the manager shook hands with him.

'Mr Foreman, I wanted to have a talk to you about the money you've got on deposit with us. D'you know exactly how much it is?'

'Not within a pound or two, sir; but I've got a pretty rough idea.'

'Apart from what you paid in this morning it's a little over thirty thousand pounds. That's a very large sum to have on deposit and I should have thought you'd do better to invest it.'

'I wouldn't want to take no risk, sir. I know it's safe in the bank.'

'You needn't have the least anxiety. We'll make you out a list of absolutely gilt-edged securities. They'll bring you in a better rate of interest than we can possibly afford to give you.'

A troubled look settled on Mr Foreman's distinguished face. 'I've never 'ad anything to do with stocks and shares and I'd 'ave to leave it all in your 'ands,' he said.

The manager smiled. 'We'll do everything. All you'll have to do next time you come in is just to sign the transfers.'

'I could do that all right,' said Albert uncertainly. 'But 'ow should I know what I was signin'?'

'I suppose you can read,' said the manager a trifle sharply.

Mr Foreman gave him a disarming smile.

'Well, sir, that's just it. I can't. I know it sounds funny-like, but there it is, I can't read or write, only me name, an' I only learnt to do that when I went into business.'

The manager was so surprised that he jumped up from his chair.

'That's the most extraordinary thing I ever heard.'

'You see, it's like this, sir, I never 'ad the opportunity until it was too late and then some'ow I wouldn't. I got obstinate-like.'

The manager stared at him as though he were a prehistoric monster.

'And do you mean to say that you've built up this important business and amassed a fortune of thirty thousand pounds without being able to read or write? Good God, man, what would you be now if you had been able to?'

'I can tell you that, sir,' said Mr Foreman, a little smile on his still aristocratic features. 'I'd be verger of St Peter's, Neville Square.'

A Friend in Need

OR thirty years now I have been studying my fellow-men.
I do not know very much about them. I should certainly
hesitate to engage a servant on his face, and yet I suppose
it is on the face that for the most part we judge the persons we
meet. We draw our conclusions from the shape of the jaw, the
look in the eyes, the contour of the mouth. I wonder if we are
more often right than wrong. Why novels and plays are so often
untrue to life is because their authors, perhaps of necessity,
make their characters all of a piece. They cannot afford to
make them self-contradictory, for then they become incom-
prehensible, and yet self-contradictory is what most of us are.
We are a haphazard bundle of inconsistent qualities. In books
on logic they will tell you that it is absurd to say that yellow
is tubular or gratitude heavier than air; but in that mixture of
incongruities that makes up the self yellow may very well be a
horse and cart and gratitude the middle of next week. I shrug
my shoulders when people tell me that their first impressions of
a person are always right. I think they must have small insight
or great vanity. For my own part I find that the longer I know
people the more they puzzle me: my oldest friends are just
those of whom I can say that I don't know the first thing about
them.

These reflections have occurred to me because I read in this
morning's paper that Edward Hyde Burton had died at Kobe.
He was a merchant and he had been in business in Japan for
many years. I knew him very little, but he interested me be-

cause once he gave me a great surprise. Unless I had heard the story from his own lips I should never have believed that he was capable of such an action. It was more startling because both in appearance and manner he suggested a very definite type. Here if ever was a man all of a piece. He was a tiny little fellow, not much more than five feet four in height, and very slender, with white hair, a red face much wrinkled, and blue eyes. I suppose he was about sixty when I knew him. He was always neatly and quietly dressed in accordance with his age and station.

Though his offices were in Kobe Burton often came down to Yokohama. I happened on one occasion to be spending a few days there, waiting for a ship, and I was introduced to him at the British Club. We played bridge together. He played a good game and a generous one. He did not talk very much, either then or later when we were having drinks, but what he said was sensible. He had a quiet, dry humour. He seemed to be popular at the club and afterwards, when he had gone, they described him as one of the best. It happened that we were both staying at the Grand Hotel and next day he asked me to dine with him. I met his wife, fat, elderly and smiling, and his two daughters. It was evidently a united and affectionate family. I think the chief thing that struck me about Burton was his kindliness. There was something very pleasing in his mild blue eyes. His voice was gentle; you could not imagine that he could possibly raise it in anger; his smile was benign. Here was a man who attracted you because you felt in him a real love for his fellows. He had charm. But there was nothing mawkish in him: he liked his game of cards and his cocktail, he could tell with point a good and spicy story, and in his youth he had been something of an athlete. He was a rich man and he had made every penny himself. I suppose one thing that made you like him was that he was so small and frail; he aroused your instincts of protection. You felt that he could not bear to hurt a fly.

One afternoon I was sitting in the lounge of the Grand Hotel. This was before the earthquake and they had leather arm-chairs there. From the windows you had a spacious view of the harbour with its crowded traffic. There were great liners on their way to Vancouver and San Francisco or to Europe by way of Shanghai, Hong-Kong and Singapore; there were tramps of all nations, battered and sea-worn, junks with their high sterns and great coloured sails, and innumerable sampans. It was a busy, exhilarating scene, and yet, I know not why, restful to the spirit. Here was romance and it seemed that you had but to stretch out your hand to touch it.

Burton came into the lounge presently and caught sight of me. He seated himself in the chair next to mine.

'What do you say to a little drink?'

He clapped his hands for a boy and ordered two gin fizzes. As the boy brought them a man passed along the street out-side and seeing me waved his hand.

'Do you know Turner?' said Burton as I nodded a greeting. 'I've met him at the club. I'm told he's a remittance man.'

'Yes, I believe he is. We have a good many here.'

'He plays bridge well.'

'They generally do. There was a fellow here last year, oddly enough a namesake of mine, who was the best bridge player I ever met. I suppose you never came across him in London. Lenny Burton he called himself. I believe he'd belonged to some very good clubs.'

'No, I don't believe I remember the name.'

'He was quite a remarkable player. He seemed to have an instinct about the cards. It was uncanny. I used to play with him a lot. He was in Kobe for some time.'

Burton sipped his gin fizz.

'It's rather a funny story,' he said. 'He wasn't a bad chap. I liked him. He was always well-dressed and smart-looking. He was handsome in a way with curly hair and pink-and-white cheeks. Women thought a lot of him. There was no harm in him, you know, he was only wild. Of course he drank too much. Those sort of fellows always do. A bit of money used to come in for him once a quarter and he made a bit more by card-playing. He won a good deal of mine, I know that.'

Burton gave a kindly chuckle. I knew from my own experience that he could lose money at bridge with a good grace. He stroked his shaven chin with his thin hand; the veins stood out on it and it was almost transparent.

'I suppose that is why he came to me when he went broke, that and the fact that he was a namesake of mine. He came to see me in my office one day and asked me for a job. I was rather surprised. He told me that there was no more money coming from home and he wanted to work. I asked him how old he was.

' "Thirty-five," he said.

' "And what have you been doing hitherto?" I asked him.

' "Well, nothing very much," he said.

'I couldn't help laughing.

' "I'm afraid I can't do anything for you just yet," I said. "Come back and see me in another thirty-five years, and I'll see what I can do."

'He didn't move. He went rather pale. He hesitated for a moment and then he told me that he had had bad luck at cards for some time. He hadn't been willing to stick to bridge, he'd been playing poker, and he'd got trimmed. He hadn't a penny. He'd pawned everything he had. He couldn't pay his hotel bill and they wouldn't give him any more credit. He was down and out. If he couldn't get something to do he'd have to commit suicide.

'I looked at him for a bit. I could see now that he was all to pieces. He'd been drinking more than usual and he looked fifty. The girls wouldn't have thought so much of him if they'd seen him then.

' "Well, isn't there anything you can do except play cards?"
I asked him.

' "I can swim," he said.

' "Swim!"

'I could hardly believe my ears; it seemed such an insane
answer to give.

' "I swam for my university."

'I got some glimmering of what he was driving at. I've known
too many men who were little tin gods at their university to
be impressed by it.

' "I was a pretty good swimmer myself when I was a young
man," I said.

'Suddenly I had an idea.'

Pausing in his story, Burton turned to me.

'Do you know Kobe?' he asked.

'No,' I said, 'I passed through it once, but I only spent a night
there.'

'Then you don't know the Shioya Club. When I was a young
man I swam from there round the beacon and landed at the
creek of Tarumi. It's over three miles and it's rather difficult
on account of the currents round the beacon. Well, I told my
young namesake about it and I said to him that if he'd do it
I'd give him a job.

'I could see he was rather taken aback.

' "You say you're a swimmer," I said.

' "I'm not in very good condition," he answered.

'I didn't say anything. I shrugged my shoulders. He looked at
me for a moment and then he nodded.

' "All right," he said. "When do you want me to do it?"

'I looked at my watch. It was just after ten.

' "The swim shouldn't take you much over an hour and a
quarter. I'll drive round to the creek at half-past twelve and
meet you. I'll take you back to the club to dress and then we'll
have lunch together."

' "Done," he said.

'We shook hands. I wished him good luck and he left me. I had a lot of work to do that morning and I only just managed to get to the creek at Tarumi at half-past twelve. But I needn't have hurried; he never turned up.'

'Did he funk it at the last moment?' I asked.

'No, he didn't funk it. He started all right. But of course he'd ruined his constitution by drink and dissipation. The currents round the beacon were more than he could manage. We didn't get the body for about three days.'

I didn't say anything for a moment or two. I was a trifle shocked. Then I asked Burton a question.

'When you made him that offer of a job, did you know he'd be drowned?'

He gave a little mild chuckle and he looked at me with those kind and candid blue eyes of his. He rubbed his chin with his hand.

'Well, I hadn't got a vacancy in my office at the moment.'

The Kite

I KNOW this is an odd story. I don't understand it myself and if I set it down in black and white it is only with a faint hope that when I have written it I may get a clearer view of it, or rather with the hope that some reader, better acquainted with the complications of human nature than I am, may offer me an explanation that will make it comprehensible to me. Of course the first thing that occurs to me is that there is something Freudian about it. Now, I have read a good deal of Freud, and some books by his followers, and intending to write this story I have recently flipped through again the volume published by the Modern Library which contains his basic writings. It was something of a task, for he is a dull and verbose writer, and the acrimony with which he claims to have originated such and such a theory shows a vanity and a jealousy of others working in the same field which somewhat ill become the man of science. I believe, however, that he was a kindly and benign old party. As we know, there is often a great difference between the man and the writer. The writer may be bitter, harsh and brutal, while the man may be so meek and mild that he wouldn't say boo to a goose. But that is neither here nor there. I found nothing in my re-reading of Freud's works that cast any light on the subject I had in mind. I can only relate the facts and leave it at that.

First of all I must make it plain that it is not my story and that I knew none of the persons with whom it is concerned. It was told me one evening by my friend Ned Preston, and he told it me because he didn't know how to deal with the circumstances and he thought, quite wrongly as it happened, that I might be able to give him some advice that would help him. In a previous story I have related what I thought the reader should know about Ned Preston, and so now I need only remind him that my friend was a prison visitor at Wormwood Scrubs. He took his duties very seriously and made the prisoners' troubles his own. We had been dining together at the Café Royal in that long, low room with its absurd and charming decoration which is all that remains of the old Café Royal that painters have loved to paint; and we were sitting over our coffee and liqueurs and, so far as Ned was concerned against his doctor's orders, smoking very long and very good Havanas.

'I've got a funny chap to deal with at the Scrubs just now,' he said, after a pause, 'and I'm blowed if I know how to deal with him.'

'What's he in for?' I asked.

'He left his wife and the court ordered him to pay so much a week in alimony and he's absolutely refused to pay it. I've argued with him till I was blue in the face. I've told him he's only cutting off his nose to spite his face. He says he'll stay in gaol all his life rather than pay her a penny. I tell him he can't let her starve, and all he says is: "Why not?" He's perfectly well behaved, he's no trouble, he works well, he seems quite happy, he's just getting a lot of fun out of thinking what a devil of a time his wife is having.'

'What's he got against her?'

'She smashed his kite.'

'She did what?' I cried.

'Exactly that. She smashed his kite. He says he'll never forgive her for that till his dying day.'

'He must be crazy.'

'No, he isn't, he's a perfectly reasonable, quite intelligent, decent fellow.'

Herbert Sunbury was his name, and his mother, who was very refined, never allowed him to be called Herb or Bertie, but always Herbert, just as she never called her husband Sam but only Samuel. Mrs Sunbury's first name was Beatrice, and when she got engaged to Mr Sunbury and he ventured to call her Bea she put her foot down firmly.

'Beatrice I was christened,' she said, 'and Beatrice I always have been and always shall be, to you and to my nearest and dearest.'

She was a little woman, but strong, active and wiry, with a sallow skin, sharp, regular features and small, beady eyes. Her hair, suspiciously black for her age, was always very neat, and she wore it in the style of Queen Victoria's daughters, which she had adopted as soon as she was old enough to put it up and had never thought fit to change. The possibility that she did something to keep her hair its original colour was, if such was the case, her only concession to frivolity, for, far from using rouge or lipstick, she had never in her life so much as passed a powder-puff over her nose. She never wore anything but black dresses of good material, but made (by a little woman round the corner) regardless of fashion after a pattern that was both serviceable and decorous. Her only ornament was a thin gold chain from which hung a small gold cross.

Samuel Sunbury was a little man too. He was as thin and spare as his wife, but he had sandy hair, gone very thin now so that he had to wear it very long on one side and brush it carefully over the large bald patch. He had pale blue eyes and his complexion was pasty. He was a clerk in a lawyer's office and had worked his way up from office boy to a respectable position. His employer called him Mr Sunbury and sometimes asked him to see an unimportant client. Every morning for twenty-four years Samuel Sunbury had taken the same train to the City, except of course on Sundays and during his fortnight's holiday at the seaside, and every evening he had taken the same train back to the suburb in which he lived. He was neat in his dress; he went to work in quiet grey trousers, a black coat and a bowler hat, and when he came home he put on his slippers and a black coat which was too old and shiny to wear at the office; but on Sundays when he went to the chapel he and Mrs Sunbury attended he wore a morning coat with his bowler. Thus he showed his respect for the day of rest and at the same time registered a protest against the ungodly who went bicycling or lounged about the streets until the pubs opened. On principle the Sunburys were total abstainers, but on Sundays, when to make up for the frugal lunch, consisting of a scone and butter with a glass of milk, which Samuel had during the week, Beatrice gave him a good dinner of roast beef and Yorkshire pudding, for his health's sake she liked him to have a glass of beer. Since she wouldn't for the world have kept liquor in the house, he sneaked out with a jug after morning service and got a quart from the pub round the corner; but nothing would induce him to drink alone, so, just to be sociable-like, she had a glass too.

Herbert was the only child the Lord had vouchsafed to them, and this certainly through no precaution on their part. It just happened that way. They doted on him. He was a pretty baby and then a good-looking child. Mrs Sunbury brought him up carefully. She taught him to sit up at table and not put his elbows on it, and she taught him how to use his knife and fork like a little gentleman. She taught him to stretch out his little finger when he took his tea-cup to drink out of it and when he asked why, she said:

'Never you mind. That's how it's done. It shows you know what's what.'

In due course Herbert grew old enough to go to school. Mrs Sunbury was anxious because she had never let him play with the children in the street.

'Evil communications corrupt good manners,' she said. 'I

always have kept myself to myself and I always shall keep myself to myself.'

Although they had lived in the same house ever since they were married she had taken care to keep her neighbours at a distance.

'You never know who people are in London,' she said. 'One thing leads to another, and before you know where you are you're mixed up with a lot of riff-raff and you can't get rid of them.'

She didn't like the idea of Herbert being thrown into contact with a lot of rough boys at the County Council school and she said to him:

'Now, Herbert, do what I do; keep yourself to yourself and don't have anything more to do with them than you can help.'

But Herbert got on very well at school. He was a good worker and far from stupid. His reports were excellent. It turned out that he had a good head for figures.

'If that's a fact,' said Samuel Sunbury, 'he'd better be an accountant. There's always a good job waiting for a good accountant.'

So it was settled there and then that this was what Herbert was to be. He grew tall.

'Why, Herbert,' said his mother, 'soon you'll be as tall as your dad.'

By the time he left school he was two inches taller, and by the time he stopped growing he was five feet ten.

'Just the right height,' said his mother. 'Not too tall and not too short.'

He was a nice-looking boy, with his mother's regular features and dark hair, but he had inherited his father's blue eyes, and though he was rather pale his skin was smooth and clear. Samuel Sunbury had got him into the office of the accountants who came twice a year to do the accounts of his own firm and by the time he was twenty-one he was able to bring back to his mother every week quite a nice little sum. She gave him back three half-crowns for his lunches and ten shillings for pocket money, and the rest she put in the Savings Bank for him against a rainy day.

When Mr and Mrs Sunbury went to bed on the night of Herbert's twenty-first birthday, and in passing I may say that Mrs Sunbury never went to bed, she retired, but Mr Sunbury, who was not quite so refined as his wife, always said: 'Me for Bedford,' – when then Mr and Mrs Sunbury went to bed, Mrs Sunbury said:

'Some people don't know how lucky they are; thank the Lord, I do. No one's ever had a better son than our Herbert. Hardly a day's illness in his life and he's never given me a moment's worry. It just shows if you bring up somebody right they'll be a credit to you. Fancy him being twenty-one, I can hardly believe it.'

'Yes, I suppose before we know where we are he'll be marrying and leaving us.'

'What should he want to do that for?' asked Mrs Sunbury with asperity. 'He's got a good home here, hasn't he? Don't you go putting silly ideas into his head, Samuel, or you and me'll have words and you know that's the last thing I want. Marry indeed! He's got more sense than that. He knows when he's well off. He's got sense, Herbert has.'

Mr Sunbury was silent. He had long ago learnt that it didn't get him anywhere with Beatrice to answer back.

'I don't hold with a man marrying till he knows his own mind,' she went on. 'And a man doesn't know his own mind till he's thirty or thirty-five.'

'He was pleased with his presents,' said Mr Sunbury to change the conversation.

'And so he ought to be,' said Mrs Sunbury, still upset.

They had in fact been handsome. Mr Sunbury had given him a silver wrist-watch, with hands that you could see in the dark, and Mrs Sunbury had given him a kite. It wasn't by any means the first one she had given him. That was when he was seven years old, and it happened this way. There was a large common near where they lived and on Saturday afternoons when it was fine Mrs Sunbury took her husband and son for a walk there. She said it was good for Samuel to get a breath of fresh air after being cooped up in a stuffy office all the week. There were always a lot of people on the common, but Mrs Sunbury who liked to keep herself to herself kept out of their way as much as possible.

'Look at them kites, Mum,' said Herbert suddenly one day.

There was a fresh breeze blowing and a number of kites, small and large, were sailing through the air.

'*Those*, Herbert, not them,' said Mrs Sunbury.

'Would you like to go and see where they start, Herbert?' asked his father.

'Oh, yes, Dad.'

There was a slight elevation in the middle of the common and as they approached it they saw boys and girls and some men racing down it to give their kites a start and catch the wind. Sometimes they didn't and fell to the ground, but when they did they would rise, and as the owner unravelled his string go higher and higher. Herbert looked with ravishment.

'Mum, can I have a kite?' he cried.

He had already learnt that when he wanted anything it was better to ask his mother first.

'Whatever for?' she said.

'To fly it, Mum.'

'If you're so sharp you'll cut yourself,' she said.

Mr and Mrs Sunbury exchanged a smile over the little boy's head. Fancy him wanting a kite. Growing quite a little man he was.

'If you're a good boy and wash your teeth regular every morning without me telling you I shouldn't be surprised if Santa Claus didn't bring you a kite on Christmas Day.'

Christmas wasn't far off and Santa Claus brought Herbert his first kite. At the beginning he wasn't very clever at managing it, and Mr Sunbury had to run down the hill himself and start it for him. It was a very small kite, but when Herbert saw it swim through the air and felt the little tug it gave his hand he was thrilled; and then every Saturday afternoon, when his father got back from the City, he would pester his parents to hurry over to the common. He quickly learnt how to fly it, and Mr and Mrs Sunbury, their hearts swelling with pride, would watch him from the top of the knoll while he ran down and as the kite caught the breeze lengthened the cord in his hand.

It became a passion with Herbert, and as he grew older and bigger his mother bought him larger and larger kites. He grew very clever at gauging the winds and could do things with his kite you wouldn't have thought possible. There were other kite-flyers on the common, not only children, but men, and since nothing brings people together so naturally as a hobby they share it was not long before Mrs Sunbury, notwithstanding her exclusiveness, found that she, her Samuel and her son were on speaking terms with all and sundry. They would compare their respective kites and boast of their accomplishments. Sometimes Herbert, a big boy of sixteen now, would challenge another kite-flyer. Then he would manoeuvre his kite to windward of the other fellow's, allow his cord to drift against his, and by a sudden jerk bring the enemy kite down. But long before this Mr Sunbury had succumbed to his son's enthusiasm and he would often ask to have a go himself. It must have been a funny sight to see him running down the hill in his striped trousers, black coat and bowler hat. Mrs Sunbury would trot sedately behind him and when the kite was sailing free would take the cord from him and watch it as it soared. Saturday afternoon became the great day of the week for them, and when Mr Sunbury and Herbert left the house in the morning to catch their train to the City the first thing they did was to look up at the sky to see if it was flying weather. They liked best of all a gusty day, with uncertain winds, for that gave them the best chance to exercise their skill. All through the week, in the evenings, they talked about it. They were contemptuous of smaller kites than theirs and envious of bigger ones. They discussed the performances of other flyers as hotly, and as scornfully, as boxers or football-players discuss their rivals. Their ambition was to have a bigger kite than anyone else and a kite that would go higher. They had long given up a cord, for the kite they gave Herbert on his twenty-first birthday was seven feet high, and they used piano wire wound round a drum. But that did not satisfy Herbert. Somehow or other he had heard of a box-kite which had been invented by somebody, and the idea appealed to him at once. He thought he could devise something of the sort himself and since he could draw a little he set about making designs of it. He got a small model made and tried it out one afternoon, but it wasn't a success. He was a stubborn boy and he wasn't going to be beaten. Something was wrong, and it was up to him to put it right.

Then an unfortunate thing happened. Herbert began to go out after supper. Mrs Sunbury didn't like it much, but Mr Sunbury reasoned with her. After all, the boy was twenty-two, and it must be dull for him to stay home all the time. If he wanted to go for a walk or see a movie there was no great harm. Herbert had fallen in love. One Saturday evening, after they'd had a wonderful time on the common, while they were at supper, out of a clear sky he said suddenly:

'Mum, I've asked a young lady to come in to tea tomorrow. Is that all right?'

'You done what?' said Mrs Sunbury, for a moment forgetting her grammar.

'You heard, Mum.'

'And may I ask who she is and how you got to know her?'

'Her name's Bevan, Betty Bevan, and I met her first at the pictures one Saturday afternoon when it was raining. It was an accident-like. She was sitting next me and she dropped her bag and I picked it up and she said thank you and so naturally we got talking.'

'And d'you mean to tell me you fell for an old trick like that? Dropped her bag indeed!'

'You're making a mistake, Mum, she's a nice girl, she is really and well educated too.'

'And when did all this happen?'

'About three months ago.'

'Oh, you met her three months ago and you've asked her to come to tea tomorrow?'

'Well, I've seen her since of course. That first day, after the show, I asked her if she'd come to the pictures with me on the Tuesday evening, and she said she didn't know, perhaps she would and perhaps she wouldn't. But she came all right.'

'She would. I could have told you that.'

'And we've been going to the pictures about twice a week ever since.'

'So that's why you've taken to going out so often?'

'That's right. But, look, I don't want to force her on you, if you don't want her to come to tea I'll say you've got a head-ache and take her out.'

'Your mum will have her to tea all right,' said Mr Sunbury. 'Won't you, dear? It's only that your mum can't abide strangers. She never has liked them.'

'I keep myself to myself,' said Mrs Sunbury gloomily. 'What does she do?'

'She works in a typewriting office in the City and she lives at home, if you call it home; you see, her mum died and her dad married again, and they've got three kids and she doesn't get on with her step-ma. Nag, nag, nag all the time, she says.'

Mrs Sunbury arranged the tea very stylishly. She took the

knick-knacks off a little table in the sitting-room, which they never used, and put a tea-cloth on it. She got out the tea-service and the plated tea-kettle which they never used either, and she made scones, baked a cake, and cut thin bread-and-butter.

'I want her to see that we're not just nobody,' she told her Samuel.

Herbert went to fetch Miss Bevan, and Mr Sunbury intercepted them at the door in case Herbert should take her into the dining-room where normally they ate and sat. Herbert gave the tea-table a glance of surprise as he ushered the young woman into the sitting-room.

'This is Betty, Mum,' he said.

'Miss Bevan, I presume,' said Mrs Sunbury.

'That's right, but call me Betty, won't you?'

'Perhaps the acquaintance is a bit short for that,' said Mrs Sunbury with a gracious smile. 'Won't you sit down, Miss Bevan?'

Strangely enough, or perhaps not strangely at all, Betty Bevan looked very much as Mrs Sunbury must have looked at her age. She had the same sharp features and the same rather small beady eyes, but her lips were scarlet with paint, her cheeks lightly rouged and her short black hair permanently waved. Mrs Sunbury took in all this at a glance, and she reckoned to a penny how much her smart rayon dress had cost, her extravagantly high-heeled shoes and the saucy hat on her head. Her frock was very short and she showed a good deal of flesh-coloured stocking. Mrs Sunbury, disapproving of her make-up and of her apparel, took an instant dislike to her, but she had made up her mind to behave like a lady, and if she didn't know how to behave like a lady nobody did, so that at first things went well. She poured out tea and asked Herbert to give a cup to his lady friend.

'Ask Miss Bevan if she'll have some bread-and-butter or a scone, Samuel, my dear.'

'Have both,' said Samuel, handing round the two plates, in his coarse way. 'I like to see people eat hearty.'

Betty insecurely perched a piece of bread-and-butter and a scone on her saucer and Mrs Sunbury talked affably about the weather. She had the satisfaction of seeing that Betty was getting more and more ill-at-ease. Then she cut the cake and pressed a large piece on her guest. Betty took a bite at it and when she put it in her saucer it fell to the ground.

'Oh, I am sorry,' said the girl, as she picked it up.

'It doesn't matter at all, I'll cut you another piece,' said Mrs Sunbury.

'Oh, don't bother, I'm not particular. The floor's clean.'

'I hope so,' said Mrs Sunbury with an acid smile, 'but I wouldn't dream of letting you eat a piece of cake that's been on the floor. Bring it here, Herbert, and I'll give Miss Bevan some more.'

'I don't want any more, Mrs Sunbury, I don't really.'

'I'm sorry you don't like my cake. I made it specially for you.' She took a bit. 'It tastes all right to me.'

'It's not that, Mrs Sunbury, it's a beautiful cake, it's only that I'm not hungry.'

She refused to have more tea and Mrs Sunbury saw she was glad to get rid of the cup. 'I expect they have their meals in the kitchen,' she said to herself. Then Herbert lit a cigarette.

'Give us a fag, Herb,' said Betty. 'I'm simply dying for a smoke.'

Mrs Sunbury didn't approve of women smoking, but she only raised her eyebrows slightly.

'We prefer to call him Herbert, Miss Bevan,' she said.

Betty wasn't such a fool as not to see that Mrs Sunbury had been doing all she could to make her uncomfortable, and now she saw a chance to get back on her.

'I know,' she said. 'When he told me his name was Herbert

I nearly burst out laughing. Fancy calling anyone Herbert. A
scream, I call it.'

'I'm sorry you don't like the name my son was given at his
baptism. I think it's a very nice name. But I suppose it all
depends on what sort of class of people one is.'

Herbert stepped in to the rescue.

'At the office they call me Bertie, Mum.'

'Then all I can say is, they're a lot of very common men.'

Mrs Sunbury lapsed into a dignified silence and the conversation, such as it was, was maintained by Mr Sunbury and
Herbert. It was not without satisfaction that Mrs Sunbury perceived that Betty was offended. She also perceived that the girl
wanted to go, but didn't quite know how to manage it. She was
determined not to help her. Finally Herbert took the matter
into his own hands.

'Well, Betty, I think it's about time we were getting along,'
he said. 'I'll walk back with you.'

'Must you go already?' said Mrs Sunbury, rising to her feet.
'It's been a pleasure, I'm sure.'

'Pretty little thing,' said Mr Sunbury tentatively after the
young things had left.

'Pretty my foot. All that paint and powder. You take my
word for it, she'd look very different with her face washed and
without a perm. Common, that's what she is, common as
dirt.'

An hour later Herbert came back. He was angry.

'Look here, Mum, what d'you mean by treating the poor girl
like that? I was simply ashamed of you.'

'Don't talk to your mother like that, Herbert,' she flared up.
'You didn't ought to have brought a woman like that into my
house. Common, she is, common as dirt.'

When Mrs Sunbury got angry not only did her grammar
grow shaky, but she wasn't quite safe on her aitches. Herbert
took no notice of what she said.

'She said she'd never been so insulted in her life. I had a rare job pacifying her.'

'Well, she's never coming here again, I can tell you that straight.'

'That's what you think. I'm engaged to her, so put that in your pipe and smoke it.'

Mrs Sunbury gasped.

'You're not?'

'Yes, I am. I've been thinking about it for a long time, and then she was so upset tonight I felt sorry for her, so I popped the question and I had a rare job persuading her, I can tell you.'

'You fool,' screamed Mrs Sunbury. 'You fool.'

There was quite a scene then. Mrs Sunbury and her son went at it hammer and tongs, and when poor Samuel tried to intervene they both told him roughly to shut up. At last Herbert flung out of the room and out of the house and Mrs Sunbury burst into angry tears.

No reference was made next day to what had passed. Mrs Sunbury was frigidly polite to Herbert and he was sullen and silent. After supper he went out. On Saturday he told his father and mother that he was engaged that afternoon and wouldn't be able to come to the common with them.

'I dare say we shall be able to do without you,' said Mrs Sunbury grimly.

It was getting on to the time for their usual fortnight at the seaside. They always went to Herne Bay, because Mrs Sunbury said you had a nice class of people there, and for years they had taken the same lodgings. One evening, in as casual a way as he could, Herbert said:

'By the way, Mum, you'd better write and tell them I shan't be wanting my room this year. Betty and me are getting married and we're going to Southend for the honeymoon.'

For a moment there was dead silence in the room.

'Bit sudden-like isn't it, Herbert?' said Mr Sunbury uneasily.

'Well, they're cutting down at Betty's office and she's out of a job, so we thought we'd better get married at once. We've taken two rooms in Dabney Street and we're furnishing out of my Savings Bank money.'

Mrs Sunbury didn't say a word. She went deathly pale and tears rolled down her thin cheeks.

'Oh, come on, Mum, don't take it so hard,' said Herbert. 'A fellow has to marry sometime. If Dad hadn't married you, I shouldn't be here now, should I?'

Mrs Sunbury brushed her tears away with an impatient hand.

'Your dad didn't marry me; I married 'im. I knew he was steady and respectable. I knew he'd make a good 'usband and father. I've never 'ad cause to regret it and no more 'as your dad. That's right, Samuel, isn't it?'

'Right as rain, Beatrice,' he said quickly.

'You know, you'll like Betty when you get to know her. She's a nice girl, she is really. I believe you'd find you had a lot in common. You must give her a chance, Mum.'

'She's never going to set foot in this house only over my dead body.'

'That's absurd, Mum. Why, everything'll be just the same if you'll only be reasonable. I mean, we can go flying on Saturday afternoons same as we always did. Just this time I've been engaged it's been difficult. You see, she can't see what there is in kite-flying, but she'll come round to it, and after I'm married it'll be different, I mean I can come and fly with you and Dad; that stands to reason.'

'That's what you think. Well, let me tell you that if you marry that woman you're not going to fly my kite. I never gave it you, I bought it out of the housekeeping money, and it's mine, see.'

'All right then, have it your own way. Betty says it's a kid's game anyway and I ought to be ashamed of myself, flying a kite at my age.'

He got up and once more stalked angrily out of the house. A fortnight later he was married. Mrs Sunbury refused to go to the wedding and wouldn't let Samuel go either. They went for their holiday and came back. They resumed their usual round. On Saturday afternoons they went to the common by themselves and flew their enormous kite. Mrs Sunbury never mentioned her son. She was determined not to forgive him. But Mr Sunbury used to meet him on the morning train they both took and they chatted a little when they managed to get into the same carriage. One morning Mr Sunbury looked up at the sky.

'Good flying weather today,' he said.

'D'you and Mum still fly?'

'What do you think? She's getting as clever as I am. You should see her with her skirts pinned up running down the hill. I give you my word, I never knew she had it in her. Run? Why, she can run better than what I can.'

'Don't make me laugh, Dad!'

'I wonder you don't buy a kite of your own, Herbert. You've been always so keen on it.'

'I know I was. I did suggest it once, but you know what women are, Betty said: "Be your age," and oh, I don't know what all. I don't want a kid's kite, of course, and them big kites cost money. When we started to furnish Betty said it was cheaper in the long run to buy the best and so we went to one of them hire purchase places and what with paying them every month and the rent, well, I haven't got any more money than just what we can manage on. They say it doesn't cost any more to keep two than one, well, that's not my experience so far.'

'Isn't she working?'

'Well, no, she says after working for donkeys' years as you

might say, now she's married she's going to take it easy, and of course someone's got to keep the place clean and do the cooking.'

So it went on for six months, and then one Saturday afternoon when the Sunburys were as usual on the common Mrs Sunbury said to her husband:

'Did you see what I saw, Samuel?'

'I saw Herbert, if that's what you mean. I didn't mention it because I thought it would only upset you.'

'Don't speak to him. Pretend you haven't seen him.'

Herbert was standing among the idle lookers-on. He made no attempt to speak to his parents, but it did not escape Mrs Sunbury that he followed with all his eyes the flight of the big kite he had flown so often. It began to grow chilly and the Sunburys went home. Mrs Sunbury's face was brisk with malice.

'I wonder if he'll come next Saturday,' said Samuel.

'If I didn't think betting wrong I'd bet you sixpence he will, Samuel. I've been waiting for this all along.'

'You have?'

'I knew from the beginning he wouldn't be able to keep away from it.'

She was right. On the following Saturday and on every Saturday after that when the weather was fine Herbert turned up on the common. No intercourse passed. He just stood there for a while looking on and then strolled away. But after things had been going on like this for several weeks, the Sunburys had a surprise for him. They weren't flying the big kite which he was used to, but a new one, a box-kite, a small one, on the model for which he had made the designs himself. He saw it was creating a lot of interest among the other kite-flyers; they were standing round it and Mrs Sunbury was talking volubly. The first time Samuel ran down the hill with it the thing didn't rise, but flopped miserably on the ground, and Herbert clenched his hands and ground his teeth. He couldn't bear to see it fail. Mr

Sunbury climbed up the little hill again, and the second time the box-kite took the air. There was a cheer among the by-standers. After a while Mr Sunbury pulled it down and walked back with it to the hill. Mrs Sunbury went up to her son.

'Like to have a try, Herbert?'

He caught his breath.

'Yes, Mum, I should.'

'It's just a small one because they say you have to get the knack of it. It's not like the old-fashioned sort. But we've got specifications for a big one, and they say when you get to know about it and the wind's right you can go up to two miles with it.'

Mr Sunbury joined them.

'Samuel, Herbert wants to try the kite.'

Mr Sunbury handed it to him, a pleased smile on his face, and Herbert gave his mother his hat to hold. Then he raced down the hill, the kite took the air beautifully, and as he watched it rise his heart was filled with exultation. It was grand to see that little black thing soaring so sweetly, but even as he watched it he thought of the great big one they were having made. They'd never be able to manage that. Two miles in the air, Mum had said. Whew!

'Why don't you come back and have a cup of tea, Herbert,' said Mrs Sunbury, 'and we'll show you the designs for the new one they want to build for us. Perhaps you could make some suggestions.'

He hesitated. He'd told Betty he was just going for a walk to stretch his legs, she didn't know he'd been coming to the common every week, and she'd be waiting for him. But the temptation was irresistible.

'I don't mind if I do,' he said.

After tea they looked at the specifications. The kite was huge, with gadgets he had never seen before, and it would cost a lot of money.

'You'll never be able to fly it by yourselves,' he said.

'We can try.'

'I suppose you wouldn't like me to help you just at first?' he asked uncertainly.

'Mightn't be a bad idea,' said Mrs Sunbury.

It was late when he got home, much later than he thought, and Betty was vexed.

'Wherever have you been, Herb? I thought you were dead. Supper's waiting and everything.'

'I met some fellows and got talking.'

She gave him a sharp look, but didn't answer. She sulked.

After supper he suggested they should go to a movie, but she refused.

'You go if you want to,' she said. 'I don't care to.'

On the following Saturday he went again to the common and again his mother let him fly the kite. They had ordered the new one and expected to get it in three weeks. Presently his mother said to him:

'Elizabeth is here.'

'Betty?'

'Spying on you.'

It gave him a nasty turn, but he put on a bold front.

'Let her spy. I don't care.'

But he was nervous and wouldn't go back to tea with his parents. He went straight home. Betty was waiting for him.

'So that's the fellows you got talking to. I've been suspicious for some time, you going for a walk on Saturday afternoons, and all of a sudden I tumbled to it. Flying a kite, you, a grown man. Contemptible I call it.'

'I don't care what you call it. I like it, and if you don't like it you can lump it.'

'I won't have it and I tell you that straight. I'm not going to have you make a fool of yourself.'

'I've flown a kite every Saturday afternoon ever since I was a kid, and I'm going to fly a kite as long as ever I want to.'

'It's that old bitch, she's just trying to get you away from me. I know her. If you were a man you'd never speak to her again, not after the way she's treated me.'

'I won't have you call her that. She's my mother and I've got the right to see her as often as ever I want to.'

The quarrel went on hour after hour. Betty screamed at him and Herbert shouted at her. They had had trifling disagreements before, because they were both obstinate, but this was the first serious row they had had. They didn't speak to one another on the Sunday, and during the rest of the week, though outwardly there was peace between them, their ill-feeling rankled. It happened that the next two Saturdays it poured with rain. Betty smiled to herself when she saw the downpour, but if Herbert was disappointed he gave no sign of it. The recollection of their quarrel grew dim. Living in two rooms as they did, sleeping in the same bed, it was inevitable that they should agree to forget their differences. Betty went out of her way to be nice to her Herb, and she thought that now she had given him a taste of her tongue and he knew she wasn't going to be put upon by anyone, he'd be reasonable. He was a good husband in his way, generous with his money and steady. Give her time and she'd manage him all right.

But after a fortnight of bad weather it cleared.

'Looks as if we're going to have good flying weather tomorrow,' said Mr Sunbury as they met on the platform to await their morning train. 'The new kite's come.'

'It has?'

'Your mum says of course we'd like you to come and help us with it, but no one's got the right to come between a man and his wife, and if you're afraid of Betty, her kicking up a rumpus, I mean, you'd better not come. There's a young fellow we've got to know on the common who's just mad about it, and he says he'll get it to fly if anybody can.'

Herbert was seized with a pang of jealousy.

'Don't you let any strangers touch our kite. I'll be there all right.'

'Well, you think it over, Herbert, and if you don't come we shall quite understand.'

'I'll come,' said Herbert.

So next day when he got back from the City he changed from his business clothes into slacks and an old coat. Betty came into the bedroom.

'What are you doing?'

'Changing,' he answered gaily. He was so excited, he couldn't keep the secret to himself. 'Their new kite's come and I'm going to fly it.'

'Oh no, you're not,' she said. 'I won't have it.'

'Don't be a fool, Betty. I'm going, I tell you, and if you don't like it you can do the other thing.'

'I'm not going to let you, so that's that.'

She shut the door and stood in front of it. Her eyes flashed and her jaw was set. She was a little thing and he was a tall strong man. He took hold of her two arms to push her out of the way, but she kicked him violently on the shin.

'D'you want me to give you a sock on the jaw?'

'If you go you don't come back,' she shouted.

He caught her up, though she struggled and kicked, threw her on to the bed and went out.

If the small box-kite had caused an excitement on the common it was nothing to what the new one caused. But it was difficult to manage, and though they ran and panted and other enthusiastic flyers helped them Herbert couldn't get it up.

'Never mind,' he said, 'we'll get the knack of it presently. The wind's not right today, that's all.'

He went back to tea with his father and mother and they talked it over just as they had talked in the old days. He delayed going because he didn't fancy the scene Betty would make him, but when Mrs Sunbury went into the kitchen to get supper ready he had to go home. Betty was reading the paper. She looked up.

'Your bag's packed,' she said.

'My what?'

'You heard what I said. I said if you went you needn't come back. I forgot about your things. Everything's packed. It's in the bedroom.'

He looked at her for a moment with surprise. She pretended to be reading again. He would have liked to give her a good hiding.

'All right, have it your own way,' he said.

He went into the bedroom. His clothes were packed in a suitcase, and there was a brown-paper parcel in which Betty had put whatever was left over. He took the bag in one hand, the parcel in the other, walked through the sitting-room without a word and out of the house. He walked to his mother's and rang the bell. She opened the door.

'I've come home, Mum,' he said.

'Have you, Herbert? Your room's ready for you. Put your things down and come in. We were just sitting down to supper.' They went into the dining-room. 'Samuel, Herbert's come home. Run out and get a quart of beer.'

Over supper and during the rest of the evening he told them the trouble he had had with Betty.

'Well, you're well out of it, Herbert,' said Mrs Sunbury when he had finished. 'I told you she was no wife for you. Common she is, common as dirt, and you who's always been brought up so nice.'

He found it good to sleep in his own bed, the bed he'd been used to all his life, and to come down to breakfast on the Sunday morning, unshaved and unwashed, and read the *News of the World*.

'We won't go to chapel this morning,' said Mrs Sunbury.

'It's been an upset to you, Herbert; we'll all take it easy to-day.'

During the week they talked a lot about the kite, but they also talked a lot about Betty. They discussed what she would do next.

'She'll try and get you back,' said Mrs Sunbury.

'A fat chance she's got of doing that,' said Herbert.

'You'll have to provide for her,' said his father.

'Why should he do that?' cried Mrs Sunbury. 'She trapped him into marrying her and now she's turned him out of the home he made for her.'

'I'll give her what's right as long as she leaves me alone.'

He was feeling more comfortable every day, in fact he was beginning to feel as if he'd never been away, he settled in like a dog in its own particular basket; it was nice having his mother to brush his clothes and mend his socks; she gave him the sort of things he'd always eaten and liked best; Betty was a scrappy sort of cook, it had been fun just at first, like picnicking, but it wasn't the sort of eating a man could get his teeth into, and he could never get over his mother's idea that fresh food was better than the stuff you bought in tins. He got sick of the sight of tinned salmon. Then it was nice to have space to move about in rather than be cooped up in two small rooms, one of which had to serve as a kitchen as well.

'I never made a bigger mistake in my life than when I left home, Mum,' he said to her once.

'I know that, Herbert, but you're back now and you've got no cause ever to leave it again.'

His salary was paid on Friday and in the evening when they had just finished supper the bell rang.

'That's her,' they said with one voice.

Herbert went pale. His mother gave him a glance.

'You leave it to me,' she said. 'I'll see her.'

She opened the door. Betty was standing on the threshold.

She tried to push her way in, but Mrs Sunbury prevented her.

'I want to see Herb.'

'You can't. He's out.'

'No, he isn't. I watched him go in with his dad and he hasn't come out again.'

'Well, he doesn't want to see you, and if you start making a disturbance I'll call the police.'

'I want my week's money.'

'That's all you've ever wanted of him.' She took out her purse. 'There's thirty-five shillings for you.'

'Thirty-five shillings? The rent's twelve shillings a week.'

'That's all you're going to get. He's got to pay his board here, hasn't he?'

'And then there's the instalments on the furniture.'

'We'll see about that when the time comes. D'you want the money or don't you?'

Confused, unhappy, browbeaten, Betty stood irresolutely. Mrs Sunbury thrust the money in her hand and slammed the door in her face. She went back to the dining-room.

'I've settled her hash all right,' she said.

The bell rang again, it rang repeatedly, but they did not answer it, and presently it stopped. They guessed that Betty had gone away.

It was fine next day, with just the right velocity in the wind, and Herbert, after failing two or three times, found he had got the knack of flying the big box-kite. It soared into the air and up and up as he unreeled the wire.

'Why, it's a mile up if it's a yard,' he told his mother excitedly.

He had never had such a thrill in his life.

Several weeks passed by. They concocted a letter for Herbert to write in which he told Betty that so long as she didn't molest him or members of his family she would receive a postal order for thirty-five shillings every Saturday morning and he would pay the instalments on the furniture as they came due. Mrs Sunbury had been much against this, but Mr Sunbury, for once at variance with her, and Herbert agreed that it was the right thing to do. Herbert by then had learnt the ways of the new kite and was able to do great things with it. He no longer bothered to have contests with the other kite-flyers. He was out of their class. Saturday afternoons were his moments of glory. He revelled in the admiration he aroused in the bystanders and enjoyed the envy he knew he excited in the less fortunate flyers. Then one evening when he was walking back from the station with his father Betty waylaid him.

'Hulloa, Herb,' she said.

'Hulloa.'

'I want to talk to my husband alone, Mr Sunbury.'

'There's nothing you've got to say to me that my dad can't hear,' said Herbert sullenly.

She hesitated. Mr Sunbury fidgeted. He didn't know whether to stay or go.

'All right, then,' she said. 'I want you to come back home, Herb. I didn't mean it that night when I packed your bag. I only did it to frighten you. I was in a temper. I'm sorry for what I did. It's all so silly, quarrelling about a kite.'

'Well, I'm not coming back, see. When you turned me out you did me the best turn you ever did me.'

Tears began to trickle down Betty's cheeks.

'But I love you, Herb. If you want to fly your silly old kite, you fly it, I don't care so long as you come back.'

'Thank you very much, but it's not good enough. I know when I'm well off and I've had enough of married life to last me a lifetime. Come on, Dad.'

They walked on quickly and Betty made no attempt to follow them. On the following Sunday they went to chapel and after dinner Herbert went to the coal-shed where they kept the kite to have a look at it. He just couldn't keep away from it. He doted on it. In a minute he rushed back, his face white, with a hatchet in his hand.

'She's smashed it up. She did it with this.'

The Sunburys gave a cry of consternation and hurried to the coal-shed. What Herbert had said was true. The kite, the new, expensive kite, was in fragments. It had been savagely attacked with the hatchet, the woodwork was all in pieces, the reel was hacked to bits.

'She must have done it while we were at chapel. Watched us go out, that's what she did.'

'But how did she get in?' asked Mr Sunbury.

'I had two keys. When I came home I noticed one was missing, but I didn't think anything about it.'

'You can't be sure she did it, some of them fellows on the common have been very snooty, I wouldn't put it past them to have done this.'

'Well, we'll soon find out,' said Herbert. 'I'll go and ask her, and if she did it I'll kill her.'

His rage was so terrible that Mrs Sunbury was frightened.

'And get yourself hung for murder? No, Herbert, I won't let you go. Let your dad go, and when he comes back we'll decide what to do.'

'That's right, Herbert, let me go.'

They had a job to persuade him, but in the end Mr Sunbury went. In half an hour he came back.

'She did it all right. She told me straight out. She's proud of it. I won't repeat her language, it fair startled me, but the long and short of it was she was jealous of the kite. She said Herbert loved the kite more than he loved her and so she smashed it up and if she had to do it again she'd do it again.'

'Lucky she didn't tell me that. I'd have wrung her neck even if I'd had to swing for it. Well, she never gets another penny out of me, that's all.'

'She'll sue you,' said his father.

'Let her.'

'The instalment on the furniture is due next week, Herbert,' said Mrs Sunbury quietly. 'In your place I wouldn't pay it.'

'Then they'll just take it away,' said Samuel, 'and all the money he's paid on it so far will be wasted.'

'Well, what of it?' she answered. 'He can afford it. He's rid of her for good and all and we've got him back and that's the chief thing.'

'I don't care twopence about the money,' said Herbert. 'I can see her face when they come and take the furniture away. It meant a lot to her, it did, and the piano, she set a rare store on that piano.'

So on the following Friday he did not send Betty her weekly money, and when she sent him on a letter from the furniture people to say that if he didn't pay the instalment due by such and such a date they would remove it, he wrote back and said he wasn't in a position to continue the payments and they could remove the furniture at their convenience. Betty took to waiting for him at the station, and when he wouldn't speak to her followed him down the street screaming curses at him. In the evenings she would come to the house and ring the bell till they thought they would go mad, and Mr and Mrs Sunbury had the greatest difficulty in preventing Herbert from going out and giving her a sound thrashing. Once she threw a stone and broke the sitting-room window. She wrote obscene and abusive postcards to him at his office. At last she went to the magistrate's court and complained that her husband had left her and wasn't providing for her support. Herbert received a summons. They both told their story and if the magistrate thought it a strange one he didn't say so. He tried to effect a reconciliation between them, but Herbert resolutely refused to go back to his wife. The magistrate ordered him to pay Betty twenty-five shillings a week. He said he wouldn't pay it.

'Then you'll go to prison,' said the magistrate. 'Next case.'

But Herbert meant what he said. On Betty's complaint he was brought once more before the magistrate, who asked him what reason he had for not obeying the order.

'I said I wouldn't pay her and I won't, not after she smashed my kite. And if you send me to prison I'll go to prison.'

The magistrate was stern with him this time.

'You're a very foolish young man,' he said. 'I'll give you a week to pay the arrears, and if I have any more nonsense from you you'll go to prison till you come to your senses.'

Herbert didn't pay, and that is how my friend Ned Preston came to know him and I heard the story.

'What d'you make of it?' asked Ned as he finished. 'You know, Betty isn't a bad girl. I've seen her several times, there's nothing wrong with her except her insane jealousy of Herbert's kite; and he isn't a fool by any means. In fact he's smarter than the average. What d'you suppose there is in kite-flying that makes the damned fool so mad about it?'

'I don't know,' I answered. I took my time to think. 'You see, I don't know a thing about flying a kite. Perhaps it gives him a sense of power as he watches it soaring towards the clouds and of mastery over the elements as he seems to bend the winds of heaven to his will. It may be that in some queer way he identifies himself with the kite flying so free and so high above him, and it's as it were an escape from the monotony of life. It may be that in some dim, confused way it represents an ideal of freedom and adventure. And you know, when a man once gets bitten with the virus of the ideal not all the King's doctors and not all the King's surgeons can rid him of it. But all this is very fanciful and I dare say it's just stuff and nonsense. I think you'd better put your problem before someone who knows a lot more about the psychology of the human animal than I do.'

Salvatore

I WONDER if I can do it.

I knew Salvatore first when he was a boy of fifteen with a pleasant, ugly face, a laughing mouth and carefree eyes. He used to spend the morning lying about the beach with next to nothing on and his brown body was as thin as a rail. He was full of grace. He was in and out of the sea all the time, swimming with the clumsy, effortless stroke common to the fisher boys. Scrambling up the jagged rocks on his hard feet, for except on Sundays he never wore shoes, he would throw himself into the deep water with a cry of delight. His father was a fisherman who owned his own little vineyard and Salvatore acted as nursemaid to his two younger brothers. He shouted to them to come inshore when they ventured out too far and made them dress when it was time to climb the hot, vine-clad hill for the frugal midday meal.

But boys in those Southern parts grow apace and in a little while he was madly in love with a pretty girl who lived on the Grande Marina. She had eyes like forest pools and held herself like a daughter of the Cæsars. They were affianced, but they could not marry till Salvatore had done his military service, and when he left the island which he had never left in his life before, to become a sailor in the navy of King Victor Emmanuel, he wept like a child. It was hard for one who had never been less free than the birds to be at the beck and call of others; it was harder still to live in a battleship with strangers instead of in a little white cottage among the vines; and when he was ashore, to walk in noisy, friendless cities with streets so crowded that he was frightened to cross them, when he had been used to silent paths and the mountains and the sea. I suppose it had never struck him that Ischia, which he looked at every evening (it was like a fairy island in the sunset) to see what the weather would be like next day, or Vesuvius, pearly in the dawn, had anything to do with him at all; but when he ceased to have them before his eyes he realized in some dim fashion that they were as much part of him as his hands and his feet. He was dreadfully homesick. But it was hardest of all to be parted from the girl he loved with all his passionate young heart. He wrote to her (in his childlike handwriting) long, ill-spelt letters in which he told her how constantly he thought of her and how much he longed to be back. He was sent here and there, to Spezzia, to Venice, to Bari and finally to China. Here he fell ill of some mysterious ailment that kept him in hospital for months. He bore it with the mute and uncomprehending patience of a dog. When he learnt that it was a form of rheumatism that made him unfit for further service his heart exulted, for he could go home; and he did not bother, in fact he scarcely listened, when the doctors told him that he would never again be quite well. What did he care when he was going back to the little island he loved so well and the girl who was waiting for him?

When he got into the rowing-boat that met the steamer from Naples and was rowed ashore he saw his father and mother standing on the jetty and his two brothers, big boys now, and he waved to them. His eyes searched among the crowd that waited there, for the girl. He could not see her. There was a great deal of kissing when he jumped up the steps and they all, emotional creatures, cried a little as they exchanged their greetings. He asked where the girl was. His mother told him that she did not know; they had not seen her for two or three weeks; so in the evening when the moon was shining over the

placid sea and the lights of Naples twinkled in the distance he
walked down to the Grande Marina to her house. She was sit
ting on the doorstep with her mother. He was a little shy be
cause he had not seen her for so long. He asked her if she had
not received the letter that he had written to her to say that he
was coming home. Yes, they had received a letter, and they had
been told by another of the island boys that he was ill. Yes, that
was why he was back; was it not a piece of luck? Oh, but they
had heard that he would never be quite well again. The doctors
talked a lot of nonsense, but he knew very well that now he
was home again he would recover. They were silent for a little
and then the mother nudged the girl. She did not try to soften
the blow. She told him straight out, with the blunt directness of
her race, that she could not marry a man who would never be
strong enough to work like a man. They had made up their
minds, her mother and father and she, and her father would
never give his consent.

When Salvatore went home he found that they all knew. The
girl's father had been to tell them what they had decided, but
they had lacked the courage to tell him themselves. He wept
on his mother's bosom. He was terribly unhappy, but he did not
blame the girl. A fisherman's life is hard and it needs strength
and endurance. He knew very well that a girl could not afford
to marry a man who might not be able to support her. His smile
was very sad and his eyes had the look of a dog that has been
beaten, but he did not complain, and he never said a hard word
of the girl he had loved so well. Then, a few months later, when
he had settled down to the common round, working in his
father's vineyard and fishing, his mother told him that there
was a young woman in the village who was willing to marry
him. Her name was Assunta.

'She's as ugly as the devil,' he said.

She was older than he, twenty-four or twenty-five, and she
had been engaged to a man who, while doing his military service,

had been killed in Africa. She had a little money of her own and if Salvatore married her she could buy him a boat of his own and they could take a vineyard that by a happy chance happened at that moment to be without a tenant. His mother told him that Assunta had seen him at the *festa* and had fallen in love with him. Salvatore smiled his sweet smile and said he would think about it. On the following Sunday, dressed in the stiff black clothes in which he looked so much less well than in the ragged shirt and trousers of every day, he went up to High Mass at the parish church and placed himself so that he could have a good look at the young woman. When he came down again he told his mother that he was willing.

Well, they were married and they settled down in a tiny whitewashed house in the middle of a handsome vineyard. Salvatore was now a great big husky fellow, tall and broad, but still with that ingenuous smile and those trusting, kindly eyes that he had had as a boy. He had the most beautiful manners I have ever seen in my life. Assunta was a grim-visaged female, with decided features, and she looked old for her years. But she had a good heart and she was no fool. I used to be amused by the little smile of devotion that she gave her husband when he was being very masculine and masterful; she never ceased to be touched by his gentle sweetness. But she could not bear the girl who had thrown him over, and notwithstanding Salvatore's smiling expostulations she had nothing but harsh words for her. Presently children were born to them.

It was a hard enough life. All through the fishing season towards evening he set out in his boat with one of his brothers for the fishing-grounds. It was a long pull of six or seven miles, and he spent the night catching the profitable cuttlefish. Then there was the long row back again in order to sell the catch in time for it to go on the early boat to Naples. At other times he was working in his vineyard from dawn till the heat drove him to rest and then again, when it was a trifle cooler, till dusk. Often his rheumatism prevented him from doing anything at all and then he would lie about the beach, smoking cigarettes, with a pleasant word for everyone notwithstanding the pain that racked his limbs. The foreigners who came down to bathe and saw him there said that these Italian fishermen were lazy devils.

Sometimes he used to bring his children down to give them a bath. They were both boys and at this time the elder was three and the younger less than two. They sprawled about at the water's edge stark naked and Salvatore standing on a rock would dip them in the water. The elder one bore it with stoicism, but the baby screamed lustily. Salvatore had enormous hands, like legs of mutton, coarse and hard from constant toil, but when he bathed his children, holding them so tenderly, drying them with delicate care, upon my word they were like flowers. He would seat the naked baby on the palm of his hand and hold him up, laughing a little at his smallness, and his laugh was like the laughter of an angel. His eyes then were as candid as his child's.

I started by saying that I wondered if I could do it and now I must tell you what it is that I have tried to do. I wanted to see whether I could hold your attention for a few pages while I drew for you the portrait of a man, just an ordinary fisherman who possessed nothing in the world except a quality which is the rarest, the most precious and the loveliest that anyone can have. Heaven only knows why he should so strangely and unexpectedly have possessed it. All I know is that it shone in him with a radiance that, if it had not been so unconscious and so humble, would have been to the common run of men hardly bearable. And in case you have not guessed what the quality was, I will tell you. Goodness, just goodness.

Mabel

I WAS at Pagan, in Burma, and from there I took the steamer to Mandalay, but a couple of days before I got there, when the boat tied up for the night at a riverside village, I made up my mind to go ashore. The skipper told me that there was there a pleasant little club in which I had only to make myself at home; they were quite used to having strangers drop off like that from the steamer, and the secretary was a very decent chap; I might even get a game of bridge. I had nothing in the world to do, so I got into one of the bullock-carts that were waiting at the landing-stage and was driven to the club. There was a man sitting on the veranda and as I walked up he nodded to me and asked whether I would have a whisky and soda or a gin and bitters. The possibility that I would have nothing at all did not even occur to him. I chose the longer drink and sat down. He was a tall, thin, bronzed man, with a big moustache, and he wore khaki shorts and a khaki shirt. I never knew his name, but when we had been chatting a little while another man came in who told me he was the secretary, and he addressed my friend as George.

'Have you heard from your wife yet?' he asked him.

The other's eyes brightened.

'Yes, I had letters by this mail. She's having no end of a time.'

'Did she tell you not to fret?'

George gave a little chuckle, but was I mistaken in thinking that there was in it the shadow of a sob?

'In point of fact she did. But that's easier said than done. Of course I know she wants a holiday, and I'm glad she should have it, but it's devilish hard on a chap.' He turned to me. 'You see, this is the first time I've ever been separated from my missus, and I'm like a lost dog without her.'

'How long have you been married?'

'Five minutes.'

The secretary of the club laughed.

'Don't be a fool, George. You've been married eight years.'

After we had talked for a little, George, looking at his watch, said he must go and change his clothes for dinner and left us. The secretary watched him disappear into the night with a smile of not unkindly irony.

'We all ask him as much as we can now that he's alone,' he told me. 'He mopes so terribly since his wife went home.'

'It must be very pleasant for her to know that her husband is as devoted to her as all that.'

'Mabel is a remarkable woman.'

He called the boy and ordered more drinks. In this hospitable place they did not ask you if you would have anything; they took it for granted. Then he settled himself in his long chair and lit a cheroot. He told me the story of George and Mabel.

They became engaged when he was home on leave, and when he returned to Burma it was arranged that she should join him in six months. But one difficulty cropped up after another; Mabel's father died, the war came, George was sent to a district unsuitable for a white woman; so that in the end it was seven years before she was able to start. He made all arrangements for the marriage, which was to take place on the day of her arrival, and went down to Rangoon to meet her. On the morning on which the ship was due he borrowed a motor-car and drove along to the dock. He paced the quay.

Then, suddenly, without warning, his nerve failed him. He had not seen Mabel for seven years. He had forgotten what she was like. She was a total stranger. He felt a terrible sinking in the pit of his stomach and his knees began to wobble. He couldn't go through with it. He must tell Mabel that he was very sorry, but he couldn't, he really couldn't marry her. But how could a man tell a girl a thing like that when she had been engaged to him for seven years and had come six thousand miles to marry him? He hadn't the nerve for that either. George was seized with the courage of despair. There was a boat at the quay on the very point of starting for Singapore; he wrote a hurried letter to Mabel, and without a stick of luggage, just in the clothes he stood up in, leaped on board.

The letter Mabel received ran somewhat as follows:

Dearest Mabel, I have been suddenly called away on business and do not know when I shall be back. I think it would be much wiser if you returned to England. My plans are very uncertain. Your loving George.

But when he arrived at Singapore he found a cable waiting for him.

Quite understand. Don't worry. Love. Mabel.

Terror made him quick-witted.

'By Jove, I believe she's following me,' he said.

He telegraphed to the shipping office at Rangoon and sure enough her name was on the passenger list of the ship that was now on its way to Singapore. There was not a moment to lose. He jumped on the train to Bangkok. But he was uneasy; she would have no difficulty in finding out that he had gone to Bangkok and it was just as simple for her to take the train as it had been for him. Fortunately there was a French tramp sailing next day for Saigon. He took it. At Saigon he would be safe; it would never occur to her that he had gone there; and if it did, surely by now she would have taken the hint. It is five days' journey from Bangkok to Saigon and the boat is dirty, cramped and uncomfortable. He was glad to arrive and took a rickshaw to the hotel. He signed his name in the visitors' book and a telegram was immediately handed to him. It contained but two

words: *Love. Mabel.* They were enough to make him break into
a cold sweat.

'When is the next boat for Hong-Kong?' he asked.

Now his flight grew serious. He sailed to Hong-Kong, but
dared not stay there; he went to Manila; Manila was ominous;
he went on to Shanghai: Shanghai was nerve-racking; every
time he went out of the hotel he expected to run straight into
Mabel's arms; no, Shanghai would never do. The only thing was
to go to Yokohama. At the Grand Hotel at Yokohama a cable
awaited him.

'*So sorry to have missed you at Manila. Love. Mabel.*'

He scanned the shipping intelligence with a fevered brow.
Where was she now? He doubled back to Shanghai. This time
he went straight to the club and asked for a telegram. It was
handed to him.

'*Arriving shortly. Love. Mabel.*'

No, no, he was not so easy to catch as all that. He had already
made his plans. The Yangtse is a long river and the Yangtse was
falling. He could just about catch the last steamer that could
get up to Chungking and then no one could travel till the following spring except by junk. Such a journey was out of the question for a woman alone. He went to Hankow and from Hankow
to Ichang, he changed boats here and from Ichang through the
rapids went to Chungking. But he was desperate now, he was
not going to take any risks: there was a place called Cheng-tu,
the capital of Szechuan, and it was four hundred miles away.
It could only be reached by road, and the road was infested
with brigands. A man would be safe there.

George collected chair-bearers and coolies and set out. It was
with a sigh of relief that he saw at last the crenellated walls of
the lonely Chinese city. From those walls at sunset you could
see the snowy mountains of Tibet.

He could rest at last: Mabel would never find him there. The
consul happened to be a friend of his and he stayed with him.

He enjoyed the comfort of a luxurious house, he enjoyed his idleness after that strenuous escape across Asia, and above all he enjoyed his divine security. The weeks passed lazily one after the other.

One morning George and the consul were in the courtyard looking at some curios that a Chinese had brought for their inspection when there was a loud knocking at the great door of the Consulate. The door-man flung it open. A chair borne by four coolies entered, advanced, and was set down. Mabel stepped out. She was neat and cool and fresh. There was nothing in her appearance to suggest that she had just come in after a fortnight on the road. George was petrified. He was as pale as death. She went up to him.

'Hulloa, George, I was so afraid I'd missed you again.'

'Hulloa, Mabel,' he faltered.

He did not know what to say. He looked this way and that: she stood between him and the doorway. She looked at him with a smile in her blue eyes.

'You haven't altered at all,' she said. 'Men can go off so dreadfully in seven years and I was afraid you'd got fat and bald. I've been so nervous. It would have been terrible if after all these years I simply hadn't been able to bring myself to marry you after all.'

She turned to George's host.

'Are you the consul?' she asked.

'I am.'

'That's all right. I'm ready to marry him as soon as I've had a bath.'

And she did.

A Marriage of Convenience

I LEFT Bangkok on a shabby little ship of four or five hundred tons. The dingy saloon, which served also as dining-room, had two narrow tables down its length with swivel chairs on both sides of them. The cabins were in the bowels of the ship and they were extremely dirty. Cockroaches walked about on the floor and however placid your temperament it is difficult not to be startled when you go to the wash-basin to wash your hands and a huge cockroach stalks leisurely out.

We dropped down the river, broad and lazy and smiling, and its green banks were dotted with little huts on piles standing at the water's edge. We crossed the bar; and the open sea, blue and still, spread before me. The look of it and the smell of it filled me with elation.

I had gone on board early in the morning and soon discovered that I was thrown amid the oddest collection of persons I had ever encountered. There were two French traders and a Belgian colonel, an Italian tenor, the American proprietor of a circus with his wife, and a retired French official with his. The circus proprietor was what is termed a good mixer, a type which according to your mood you fly from or welcome, but I happened to be feeling much pleased with life and before I had been on board an hour we had shaken for drinks, and he had shown me his animals. He was a very short fat man and his stengah-shifter, white but none too clean, outlined the noble proportions of his abdomen, but the collar was so tight that you wondered he did not choke. He had a red, clean-shaven face, a merry blue eye and short, untidy sandy hair. He wore a battered topee well on the back of his head. His name was Wilkins and he was born in Portland, Oregon. It appears that the Oriental has a passion for the circus and Mr Wilkins for twenty years had been travelling up and down the East from Port Said to Yokohama (Aden, Bombay, Madras, Calcutta, Rangoon, Singapore, Penang, Bangkok, Saigon, Huë, Hanoi, Hong-Kong, Shanghai, their names roll on the tongue savourily, crowding the imagination with sunshine and strange sounds and a multi-coloured activity) with his menagerie and his merry-go-rounds. It was a strange life he led, unusual and one that, one would have thought, must offer the occasion for all sorts of curious experiences, but the odd thing about him was that he was a perfectly commonplace little man and you would have been prepared to find him running a garage or keeping a third-rate hotel in a second-rate town in California. The fact is, and I have noticed it so often that I do not know why it should always surprise me, that the extraordinariness of a man's life does not make him extraordinary, but contrariwise if a man is extraordinary he will make extraordinariness out of a life as humdrum as that of a country curate. I wish I could feel it reasonable to tell here the story of the hermit I went to see on an island in the Torres Straits, a shipwrecked mariner who had lived there alone for thirty years, but when you are writing a book you are imprisoned by the four walls of your subject and though for the entertainment of my own digressing mind I set it down now I should be forced in the end, by my sense of what is fit to go between two covers and what is not, to cut it out. Anyhow, the long and short of it is that notwithstanding his long and intimate communion with nature and his thoughts the man was as dull, insensitive and vulgar an oaf at the end of this experience as he must have been at the beginning.

The Italian singer passed us and Mr Wilkins told me that he was a Neapolitan who was on his way to Hong-Kong to rejoin his company, which he had been forced to leave owing to an attack of malaria in Bangkok. He was an enormous fellow, and very fat, and when he flung himself into a chair it creaked with dismay. He took off his topee, displayed a great head of long, curly, greasy hair, and ran podgy and beringed fingers through it.

'He ain't very sociable,' said Mr Wilkins. 'He took the cigar I gave him, but he wouldn't have a drink. I shouldn't wonder if there wasn't somethin' rather queer about him. Nasty-lookin' guy, ain't he?'

Then a little fat woman in white came on deck holding by the hand a Wa-Wa monkey. It walked solemnly by her side.

'This is Mrs Wilkins,' said the circus proprietor, 'and our youngest son. Draw up a chair, Mrs Wilkins, and meet this gentleman. I don't know his name, but he's already paid for two drinks for me and if he can't shake any better than he has yet he'll pay for one for you too.'

Mrs Wilkins sat down with an abstracted, serious look, and with her eyes on the blue sea suggested that she did not see why she shouldn't have a lemonade.

'My, it's hot,' she murmured, fanning herself with the topee which she took off.

'Mrs Wilkins feels the heat,' said her husband. 'She's had twenty years of it now.'

'Twenty-two and a half,' said Mrs Wilkins, still looking at the sea.

'And she's never got used to it yet.'

'Nor never shall and you know it,' said Mrs Wilkins.

She was just the same size as her husband and just as fat, and she had a round red face like his and the same sandy, untidy hair. I wondered if they had married because they were so exactly alike, or if in the course of years they had acquired this astonishing resemblance. She did not turn her head but continued to look absently at the sea.

'Have you shown him the animals?' she asked.

'You bet your life I have.'

'What did he think of Percy?'

'Thought him fine.'

I could not but feel that I was being unduly left out of a conversation of which I was at all events partly the subject, so I
asked:

'Who's Percy?'

'Percy's our eldest son. There's a flyin'-fish, Elmer. He's the
oran-utan. Did he eat his food well this morning?'

'Fine. He's the biggest oran-utan in captivity. I wouldn't take
a thousand dollars for him.'

'And what relation is the elephant?' I asked.

Mrs Wilkins did not look at me, but with her blue eyes still
gazed indifferently at the sea.

'He's no relation,' she answered. 'Only a friend.'

The boy brought lemonade for Mrs Wilkins, a whisky and
soda for her husband and a gin and tonic for me. We shook
dice and I signed the chit.

'It must come expensive if he always loses when he shakes,'
Mrs Wilkins murmured to the coastline.

'I guess Egbert would like a sip of your lemonade, my dear,'
said Mr Wilkins.

Mrs Wilkins slightly turned her head and looked at the
monkey sitting on her lap.

'Would you like a sip of Mother's lemonade, Egbert?'

The monkey gave a little squeak and putting her arm round
him she handed him a straw. The monkey sucked up a little
lemonade and having drunk enough sank back against Mrs
Wilkins's ample bosom.

'Mrs Wilkins thinks the world of Egbert,' said her husband.
'You can't wonder at it, he's her youngest.'

Mrs Wilkins took another straw and thoughtfully drank her
lemonade.

'Egbert's all right,' she remarked. 'There's nothin' wrong with Egbert.'

Just then the French official, who had been sitting down, got up and began walking up and down. He had been accompanied on board by the French minister at Bangkok, one or two secretaries and a prince of the royal family. There had been a great deal of bowing and shaking of hands and as the ship slipped away from the quay much waving of hats and handkerchiefs. He was evidently a person of consequence. I had heard the captain address him as Monsieur le Gouverneur.

'That's the big noise on this boat,' said Mr Wilkins. 'He was Governor of one of the French colonies and now he's makin' a tour of the world. He came to see my circus at Bangkok. I guess I'll ask him what he'll have. What shall I call him, my dear?'

Mrs Wilkins slowly turned her head and looked at the Frenchman, with the rosette of the Legion of Honour in his buttonhole, pacing up and down.

'Don't call him anythin',' she said. 'Show him a hoop and he'll jump right through it.'

I could not but laugh. Monsieur le Gouverneur was a little man, well below the average height, and smally made, with a very ugly little face and thick, almost negroid features; and he had a bushy grey head, bushy grey eyebrows and a bushy grey moustache. He did look a little like a poodle and he had the poodle's soft, intelligent and shining eyes. Next time he passed us Mr Wilkins called out:

'*Monsoo. Qu'est ce que vous prenez?*' I cannot reproduce the eccentricities of his accent. '*Une petite verre de porto.*' He turned to me. 'Foreigners, they all drink porto. You're always safe with that.'

'Not the Dutch,' said Mrs Wilkins, with a look at the sea. 'They won't touch nothin' but Schnapps.'

The distinguished Frenchman stopped and looked at Mr

Wilkins with some bewilderment. Whereupon Mr Wilkins tapped his breast and said:

'*Moa, proprietarre Cirque. Vous avez visité.*'

Then, for a reason that escaped me, Mr Wilkins made his arms into a hoop and outlined the gestures that represented a poodle jumping through it. Then he pointed at the Wa-Wa that Mrs Wilkins was still holding on her lap.

'*La petit fils de mon femme,*' he said.

Light broke upon the Governor and he burst into a peculiarly musical and infectious laugh. Mr Wilkins began laughing too.

'*Oui, oui,*' he cried. '*Moa,* circus proprietor. *Une petite verre de porto. Oui. Oui. N'est ce pas?*'

'Mr Wilkins talks French like a Frenchman,' Mrs Wilkins informed the passing sea.

'*Mais très volontiers,*' said the Governor, still smiling. I drew him up a chair and he sat down with a bow to Mrs Wilkins.

'Tell poodle-face his name's Egbert,' she said, looking at the sea.

I called the boy and we ordered a round of drinks.

'You sign the chit, Elmer,' she said. 'It's not a bit of good Mr What's-his-name shakin' if he can't shake nothin' better than a pair of treys.'

'*Vous comprenez le français, madame?*' asked the Governor politely.

'He wants to know if you speak French, my dear.'

'Where does he think I was raised? Naples?'

Then the Governor, with exuberant gesticulation, burst into a torrent of English so fantastic that it required all my knowledge of French to understand what he was talking about.

Presently Mr Wilkins took him down to look at his animals and a little later we assembled in the stuffy saloon for luncheon. The Governor's wife appeared and was put on the captain's right. The Governor explained to her who we all were and she gave us a gracious bow. She was a large woman, tall and of a

robust build, of fifty-five perhaps, and she was dressed somewhat severely in black silk. On her head she wore a huge round
topee. Her features were so large and regular, her form so
statuesque, that you were reminded of the massive females who
take part in processions. She would have admirably suited the
role of Columbia or Britannia in a patriotic demonstration. She
towered over her diminutive husband like a skyscraper over a
shack. He talked incessantly, with vivacity and wit, and when
he said anything amusing her heavy features relaxed into a
large, fond smile.

'*Que tu es bête, mon ami,*' she said. She turned to the captain.
'You must not pay any attention to him. He is always like that.'

We had indeed a very amusing meal and when it was over we
separated to our various cabins to sleep away the heat of the
afternoon. In such a small ship having once made the acquaintance of my fellow passengers, it would have been impossible,
even had I wished it, not to pass with them every moment of
the day that I was not in my cabin. The only person who held
himself aloof was the Italian tenor. He spoke to no one, but sat
by himself as far forward as he could get, twanging a guitar in
an undertone so that you had to strain your ears to catch the
notes. We remained in sight of land and the sea was like a pail
of milk. Talking of one thing and another we watched the day
decline, we dined, and then we sat out again on deck under the
stars. The two traders played piquet in the hot saloon, but the
Belgian colonel joined our little group. He was shy and fat and
opened his mouth only to utter a civility. Soon, influenced perhaps by the night and encouraged by the darkness that gave
him, up there in the bows, the sensation of being alone with
the sea, the Italian tenor, accompanying himself on his guitar,
began to sing, first in a low tone, and then a little louder, till
presently, his music captivating him, he sang with all his might.
He had the real Italian voice, all macaroni, olive oil and sunshine, and he sang the Neapolitan songs that I had heard in my

youth in the Piazza San Ferdinando, and fragments from *La Bohème*, and *Traviata* and *Rigoletto*. He sang with emotion and false emphasis and his tremolo reminded you of every third-rate Italian tenor you had ever heard, but there in the openness of that lovely night his exaggerations only made you smile and you could not but feel in your heart a lazy sensual pleasure. He sang for an hour, perhaps, and we all fell silent; then he was still, but he did not move and we saw his huge bulk dimly outlined against the luminous sky.

I saw that the little French Governor had been holding the hand of his large wife and the sight was absurd and touching.

'Do you know that this is the anniversary of the day on which I first saw my wife?' he said, suddenly breaking the silence which had certainly weighed on him, for I had never met a more loquacious creature. 'It is also the anniversary of the day on which she promised to be my wife. And, which will surprise you, they were one and the same.'

'*Voyons, mon ami*,' said the lady, 'you are not going to bore our friends with that old story. You are really quite insupportable.'

But she spoke with a smile on her large, firm face, and in a tone that suggested that she was quite willing to hear it again.

'But it will interest them, *mon petit chou*.' It was in this way that he always addressed his wife and it was funny to hear this imposing and even majestic lady thus addressed by her small husband. 'Will it not, *monsieur*?' he asked me. 'It is a romance and who does not like romance, especially on such a night as this?'

I assured the Governor that we were all anxious to hear and the Belgian colonel took the opportunity once more to be polite.

'You see, ours was a marriage of convenience pure and simple.'

'*C'est vrai*,' said the lady. 'It would be stupid to deny it. But sometimes love comes after marriage and not before, and then it is better. It lasts longer.'

I could not but notice that the Governor gave her hand an affectionate little squeeze.

'You see, I had been in the navy, and when I retired I was forty-nine. I was strong and active and I was very anxious to find an occupation. I looked about; I pulled all the strings I could. Fortunately I had a cousin who had some political importance. It is one of the advantages of democratic government that if you have sufficient influence, merit, which otherwise might pass unnoticed, generally receives its due reward.'

'You are modesty itself, *mon pauvre ami*,' said she.

'And presently I was sent for by the Minister to the Colonies and offered the post of Governor in a certain colony. It was a very distant spot that they wished to send me to and a lonely one, but I had spent my life wandering from port to port, and that was not a matter that troubled me. I accepted with joy. The minister told me that I must be ready to start in a month. I told him that would be easy for an old bachelor who had nothing much in the world but a few clothes and a few books.

' "*Comment, mon lieutenant*," he cried. "You are a bachelor?"

' "Certainly," I answered. "And I have every intention of remaining one."

' "In that case I am afraid I must withdraw my offer. For this position it is essential that you should be married."

'It is too long a story to tell you, but the gist of it was that owing to the scandal my predecessor, a bachelor, had caused by having native girls to live in the Residency and the consequent complaints of the white people, planters and the wives of functionaries, it had been decided that the next Governor must be a model of respectability. I expostulated. I argued. I recapitulated my services to the country and the services my cousin could render at the next elections. Nothing would serve. The minister was adamant.

' "But what can I do?" I cried with dismay.

' "You can marry," said the minister.

' "*Mais voyons, monsieur le ministre*, I do not know any women. I am not a ladies' man and I am forty-nine. How do you expect me to find a wife?"

' "Nothing is more simple. Put an advertisement in the paper."

'I was confounded. I did not know what to say.

' "Well, think it over," said the minister. "If you can find a wife in a month you can go, but no wife no job. That is my last word." He smiled a little, to him the situation was not without humour. "And if you think of advertising I recommend the *Figaro*."

'I walked away from the ministry with death in my heart. I knew the place to which they desired to appoint me and I knew it would suit me very well to live there; the climate was tolerable and the Residency was spacious and comfortable. The notion of being a Governor was far from displeasing me and, having nothing much but my pension as a naval officer, the salary was not to be despised. Suddenly I made up my mind. I walked to the offices of the *Figaro*, composed an advertisement and handed it in for insertion. But I can tell you, when I walked up the Champs Elysées afterwards my heart was beating much more furiously than it had ever done when my ship was stripped for action.'

The Governor leaned forward and put his hand impressively on my knee.

'*Mon cher monsieur*, you will never believe it, but I had four thousand three hundred and seventy-two replies. It was an avalanche. I had expected half a dozen; I had to take a cab to take the letters to my hotel. My room was swamped with them. There were four thousand three hundred and seventy-two women who were willing to share my solitude and be a Governor's lady. It was staggering. They were of all ages from seventeen to seventy. There were maidens of irreproachable ancestry and the highest culture, there were unmarried ladies who had made a little slip at one period of their career and now desired to regularize their situation; there were widows whose husbands had died in the most harrowing circumstances; and there were widows whose children would be a solace to my old age. They were blonde and dark, tall and short, fat and thin; some could speak five languages and others could play the piano. Some offered me love and some craved for it; some could only give me a solid friendship but mingled with esteem; some had a fortune and others golden prospects. I was overwhelmed. I was bewildered. At last I lost my temper, for I am a passionate man, and I got up and I stamped on all those letters and all those photographs and I cried: I will marry none of them. It was hopeless, I had less than a month now and I could not see over four thousand aspirants to my hand in that time. I felt that if I did not see them all, I should be tortured for the rest of my life by the thought that I had missed the one woman the fates had destined to make me happy. I gave it up as a bad job.

'I went out of my room hideous with all those photographs and littered papers and to drive care away went on to the boulevard and sat down at the Café de la Paix. After a time I saw a friend passing and he nodded to me and smiled. I tried to smile but my heart was sore. I realized that I must spend the years that remained to me in a cheap *pension* at Toulon or Brest as an *officier de marine en retraite*. Zut! My friend stopped and coming up to me sat down.

' "What is making you look so glum, *mon cher?*" he asked me. "You who are the gayest of mortals."

'I was glad to have someone in whom I could confide my troubles and told him the whole story. He laughed consumedly. I have thought since that perhaps the incident had its comic side, but at the time, I assure you, I could see in it nothing to laugh at. I mentioned the fact to my friend not without asperity and then, controlling his mirth as best he could, he said to me:

"But, my dear fellow, do you really want to marry?" At this I entirely lost my temper.

' "You are completely idiotic," I said. "If I did not want to marry, and what is more marry at once, within the next fortnight, do you imagine that I should have spent three days reading love letters from women I have never set eyes on?"

' "Calm yourself and listen to me," he replied. "I have a cousin who lives in Geneva. She is Swiss, *du reste*, and she belongs to a family of the greatest respectability in the republic. Her morals are without reproach, she is of a suitable age, a spinster, for she has spent the last fifteen years nursing an invalid mother who has lately died, she is well educated and *pardessus le marché* she is not ugly."

' "It sounds as though she were a paragon," I said.

' "I do not say that, but she has been well brought up and would become the position you have to offer her."

' "There is one thing you forget. What inducement would there be for her to give up her friends and her accustomed life to accompany in exile a man of forty-nine who is by no means a beauty?" '

Monsieur le Gouverneur broke off his narrative and, shrugging his shoulders so emphatically that his head almost sank between them, turned to us.

'I am ugly. I admit it. I am of an ugliness that does not inspire terror or respect, but only ridicule, and that is the worst ugliness of all. When people see me for the first time they do not shrink with horror, there would evidently be something flattering in that, they burst out laughing. Listen, when the admirable Mr Wilkins showed me his animals this morning, Percy, the oran-utan, held out his arms and but for the bars of the cage would have clasped me to his bosom as a long lost brother. Once indeed when I was at the Jardin des Plantes in Paris and was told that one of the anthropoid apes had escaped I made my way to the exit as quickly as I could in fear that, mistaking me for the refugee, they would seize me and, notwithstanding my ex-postulations, shut me up in the monkey house.'

'Voyons, mon ami,' said Madame his wife, in her deep slow voice, 'you are talking even greater nonsense than usual. I do not say that you are an Apollo, in your position it is unnecessary that you should be, but you have dignity, you have poise, you are what any woman would call a fine man.'

'I will resume my story. When I made this remark to my friend he replied: "One can never tell with women. There is something about marriage that wonderfully attracts them. There would be no harm in asking her. After all it is regarded as a compliment by a woman to be asked in marriage. She can but refuse."

' "But I do not know your cousin and I do not see how I am to make her acquaintance. I cannot go to her house, ask to see her and when I am shown into the drawing-room say: Voilà, I have come to ask you to marry me. She would think I was a lunatic and scream for help. Besides, I am a man of an extreme timidity, and I could never take such a step."

' "I will tell you what to do," said my friend. "Go to Geneva and take her a box of chocolates from me. She will be glad to have news of me and will receive you with pleasure. You can have a little talk and then if you do not like the look of her you take your leave and no harm is done. If on the other hand you do, we can go into the matter and you can make a formal demand for her hand."

'I was desperate. It seemed the only thing to do. We went to a shop at once and bought an enormous box of chocolates and that night I took the train to Geneva. No sooner had I arrived than I sent her a letter to say that I was the bearer of a gift from her cousin and much wished to give myself the pleasure of delivering it in person. Within an hour I received her reply to the effect that she would be pleased to receive me at four o'clock in the afternoon. I spent the interval before my mirror and seventeen times I tied and retied my tie. As the clock struck four I presented myself at the door of her house and was immediately ushered into the drawing-room. She was waiting for me. Her cousin said she was not ugly. Imagine my surprise to see a young woman, *enfin* a woman still young, of a noble presence, with the dignity of Juno, the features of Venus, and in her expression the intelligence of Minerva.'

'You are too absurd,' said Madame. 'But by now these gentle-men know that one cannot believe all you say.'

'I swear to you that I do not exaggerate. I was so taken aback that I nearly dropped the box of chocolates. But I said to my-self: *La garde meurt mais ne se rend pas.* I presented the box of chocolates. I gave her news of her cousin. I found her amiable. We talked for a quarter of an hour. And then I said to myself: *Allons-y.* I said to her:

' "Mademoiselle, I must tell you that I did not come here merely to give you a box of chocolates."

'She smiled and remarked that evidently I must have had reasons to come to Geneva of more importance than that.

' "I came to ask you to do me the honour of marrying me."

'She gave a start.

' "But, monsieur, you are mad," she said.

' "I beseech you not to answer till you have heard the facts," I interrupted, and before she could say another word I told her the whole story. I told her about my advertisement in the *Figaro* and she laughed till the tears ran down her face. Then I repeated my offer.

' "You are serious?" she asked.

' "I have never been more serious in my life."

' "I will not deny that your offer has come as a surprise. I had not thought of marrying, I have passed the age; but evidently your offer is not one that a woman should refuse without con-sideration. I am flattered. Will you give me a few days to reflect?"

' "Mademoiselle, I am absolutely desolated," I replied. "But I have not time. If you will not marry me I must go back to Paris and resume my perusal of the fifteen or eighteen hundred letters that still await my attention."

' "It is quite evident that I cannot possibly give you an answer at once. I had not set eyes on you a quarter of an hour ago. I must consult my friends and my family."

' "What have they got to do with it? You are of full age. The matter is pressing. I cannot wait. I have told you every-thing. You are an intelligent woman. What can prolonged re-flection add to the impulse of the moment?"

' "You are not asking me to say yes or no this very minute? That is outrageous."

' "That is exactly what I am asking. My train goes back to Paris in a couple of hours."

'She looked at me reflectively.

' "You are quite evidently a lunatic. You ought to be shut up both for your own safety and that of the public."

' "Well, which is it to be?" I said. "Yes or no?"

'She shrugged her shoulders.

' "*Mon Dieu*." She waited a minute and I was on tenterhooks. "Yes."

The Governor waved his hand towards his wife.

'And there she is. We were married in a fortnight and I be-came Governor of a colony. I married a jewel, my dear sirs, a woman of the most charming character, one in a thousand, a woman of a masculine intelligence and a feminine sensibility, an admirable woman.'

'But hold your tongue, *mon ami*,' his wife said. 'You are making me as ridiculous as yourself.'

He turned to the Belgian colonel.

'Are you a bachelor, *mon colonel*? If so I strongly recom-mend you to go to Geneva. It is a nest (*une pépinière* was the word be used) of the most adorable young women. You will find a wife there as nowhere else. Geneva is besides a charming city. Do not waste a minute, but go there and I will give you a letter to my wife's nieces.'

It was she who summed up the story.

'The fact is that in a marriage of convenience you expect less and so you are less likely to be disappointed. As you do not make senseless claims on one another there is no reason for exasperation. You do not look for perfection and so you are tolerant to one another's faults. Passion is all very well, but it is not a proper foundation for marriage. *Voyez-vous*, for two people to be happy in marriage they must be able to respect one another, they must be of the same condition and their interests must be alike; then if they are decent people and are willing to give and take, to live and let live, there is no reason why their union should not be as happy as ours.' She paused. 'But, of course, my husband is a very, very remarkable man.'

Glossary

F = French G = German L = Latin S = Spanish